Acclaim For [obscured by sticker]

LAWRENCE BLOCK!

"Lawrence Block is a master of entertainment."
—*Washington Post Book World*

"The narrative is layered with detail, the action is handled with Block's distinctive clarity of style and the ending is a stunning tour de force."
—*The New York Times*

"No one writes the hard-boiled thriller better than Lawence Block."
—*San Diego Union*

"Brilliant...For clean, close-to-the-bone prose, the line goes from Dashiell Hammett to James M. Cain to Lawrence Block. He's that good."
—*Martin Cruz Smith*

"Wonderful."
—*USA Today*

"The reader is riveted to the words, the action."
—*Robert Ludlum*

"Lawrence Block is addictive. Make room on your bookshelf."
—*David Morrell*

"Block knows how to pace a story and tighten the noose of suspense. He writes sharp dialogue and knows his mean streets of New York."

—*San Francisco Examiner*

"Stellar…a master storyteller in top form."

—*Publishers Weekly*

"One of the very best writers now working the beat."

—*The Wall Street Journal*

"Block is awfully good, with an ear for dialogue, an eye for lowlife types and a gift for fast and effortless story-telling that bear comparison to Elmore Leonard."

—*Los Angeles Times*

"Lawrence Block is a master of crime fiction."

—*Jonathan Kellerman*

"Exceptional…A whale of a knockout punch to the solar plexus."

—*The New York Daily News*

"Remarkable…the suspense is relentless."

—*Philadelphia Inquirer*

"If Lawrence Block writes it, I read it."

—*Mike Lupica, New York Newsday*

"A superior storyteller."

—*San Antonio Express-News*

"Lawrence Block is one of America's best crime writers, and he has never been better."

—*The San Diego Union Book Review*

"A smooth, chilling suspense novel that stretches nerves wire-tight before they snap."

—*The Boston Herald*

"Lawrence Block is finally getting the attention he deserved."

—*Chicago Tribune*

"Ratchets up the suspense with breathtaking results as only a skilled, inventive and talented writer can do."

—*Orlando Sentinel*

"A muscular zenith piece, featuring some sharp insights into the darker side of the human condition."

—*January Magazine*

"Block's extraordinary skill as a writer is evident in the way he...spins his story with such cunning ability that you can't help being drawn into his web. The suspense is acute enough to make you hold your breath."

—*Milwaukee Journal Sentinel*

"[Block is] just too damn readable, not to mention addictive."

—*Entertainment Weekly*

"He is simply the best at what he does...If you haven't read him before, you've wasted a lot of time. Begin now."

—*Mostly Murder*

There was a knock at the door. I opened it and the room became perceptibly warmer.

Joyce wore a tan sweater and a dark brown skirt. Her green eyes were hard and soft at once—emeralds one moment and card-table felt the next. She drew the door shut behind her, then stepped past me and crossed the room to the bed. She sat on it, tucking a long leg beneath herself.

"You look puzzled," she said.

"I am."

"Why?"

"Because I don't know who you are," I said. "You sat down at the table last night and spotted some of the smoothest card manipulation anybody's likely to see anywhere. You called me on it without letting anybody know you tipped to me. And you let me take close to three yards out of the game without saying a word. I don't get it."

She opened her purse, withdrew a flat silver case. She took out a cork-tipped cigarette and put it between her red lips. Just sitting there, she managed to give off more sexuality than a stripper in Baltimore. I struck a match to give her a light and she took hold of my wrist to steady the flame. Her fingers pressed harder than they had to and her eyes held mine. Something happened, with electricity in it. I couldn't look away from her.

Joyce said, "Who do you think I am, Bill?"

I crossed to the dresser and stared at her reflection in the mirror. They say that for every man there's a woman somewhere in the world who can make him jump through fiery hoops just by snapping her fingers. They say a man's lucky if he never meets that woman.

All of a sudden I knew what they meant...

OTHER HARD CASE CRIME BOOKS YOU WILL ENJOY:

GRIFTER'S GAME *by Lawrence Block*
FADE TO BLONDE *by Max Phillips*
TOP OF THE HEAP *by Erle Stanley Gardner*
LITTLE GIRL LOST *by Richard Aleas*
TWO FOR THE MONEY *by Max Allan Collins*
THE CONFESSION *by Domenic Stansberry*
HOME IS THE SAILOR *by Day Keene*
KISS HER GOODBYE *by Allan Guthrie*
361 *by Donald E. Westlake*
PLUNDER OF THE SUN *by David Dodge*
BRANDED WOMAN *by Wade Miller*
DUTCH UNCLE *by Peter Pavia*
THE COLORADO KID *by Stephen King*
THE GIRL WITH THE LONG GREEN HEART *by Lawrence Block*
THE GUTTER AND THE GRAVE *by Ed McBain*
NIGHT WALKER *by Donald Hamilton*
A TOUCH OF DEATH *by Charles Williams*
SAY IT WITH BULLETS *by Richard Powell*
WITNESS TO MYSELF *by Seymour Shubin*
BUST *by Ken Bruen and Jason Starr*
STRAIGHT CUT *by Madison Smartt Bell*
LEMONS NEVER LIE *by Richard Stark*
THE LAST QUARRY *by Max Allan Collins*
THE GUNS OF HEAVEN *by Pete Hamill*
THE LAST MATCH *by David Dodge*
GRAVE DESCEND *by John Lange*
THE PEDDLER *by Richard S. Prather*

LUCKY *at* CARDS

by **Lawrence Block**

CRIME NOVEL

A HARD CASE CRIME BOOK
(HCC-028)
February 2007

Published by

Dorchester Publishing Co., Inc.
200 Madison Avenue
New York, NY 10016

in collaboration with Winterfall LLC

ISBN 0-8439-5768-9
ISBN-13 978-0-8439-5768-9

Cover design by Cooley Design Lab

Typeset by Swordsmith Productions

 Hard Case Crime books are selected and edited by Charles Ardai.

Printed in the United States of America

Visit us on the web at www.HardCaseCrime.com

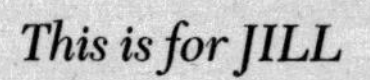
This is for JILL

LUCKY AT CARDS

I

If it hadn't been for the dentist, I would have headed on out of town. The guy had a two-room office in the old medical building on the main drag, and I saw him Monday and Wednesday and Friday of the first week I spent in town. It took him that long to cap a pair of incisors. It hurt like hell, but by the time he was through I was no longer afraid to smile in public.

"You look human again," he said.

I arose from the chair and smiled at myself in the mirror above the sink. The teeth were as good as new. I turned and grinned at him.

"Now the girls won't run away," Sy Daniels said.

"You did a good job. They look great."

In his reception room I stood smoking a cigarette while he used a pencil and paper to figure out how much I owed him.

Sy Daniels was somewhere between forty-five and fifty, with rounded features and bushy eyebrows and thick glasses. The most memorable thing about him was the taste of his fingers. He smoked more than most dentists I'd ever had anything to do with, and he smoked some special Turkish blend that tasted even worse than it smelled, and by the time I had gone to him three times I dreaded the taste of his fingers as much as the filling and capping.

I was nearly finished with my cigarette when he turned around to look up at me and tell me I owed him sixty bucks. The fee seemed reasonable but hurt anyway. I dug out my wallet and counted out the bread in tens. I gave him the bills and he marked the tab paid and handed it to me. I stuffed it in a pocket and managed a smile.

"Between you and a few poker games," I said, "this wallet is getting pretty flat."

"You play poker?"

"A little," I said. "I used to lose a few bucks a week in Chicago. We had a regular game there. But I haven't been playing since I hit your fair city."

"There are plenty of games."

"If you like to play with strangers. I don't."

The dentist shook out a cigarette and offered the pack to me. I said thanks but no thanks and he lit his and smelled up the office some more. "I know what you mean," Sy said. "About playing with strangers. But if you like a friendly game, we've got a small group of fellows who meet every Friday night. There's a seat open tonight, if you're interested."

I let my eyes light up. Then I lowered them and chewed on my upper lip for a few beats. "I'd love to play," I said. "But—"

"But what?"

"Well, I wouldn't want to get in over my head. What kind of stakes do you fellows play for?"

He told me it was just a friendly game, dollar limit, dealer's choice. They played five-card stud and seven-card stud and straight draw. They had a three-raise limit, no sandbagging, no high-low, no wild cards. My eyes lit up all over again. I told him that sounded just about perfect, that I'd been afraid for a minute that the game was one of those wild table-stakes ones where you needed a few hundred dollars to sit down.

"Oh, nothing like that," Sy Daniels told me. "This is just a friendly game, Bill. I think you'll like it."

We made the arrangements. The game was at the house of somebody named Murray Rogers, a tax lawyer. Daniels was going home for dinner. He invited me to try his wife's cooking but I dodged that with a story about a dinner appointment. He mentioned a drugstore uptown and said that if I could be there around a quarter to eight he'd pick me up and run me over to the game. That was fine, I said. I shook hands with him and left.

It was time for lunch. I had a pair of hamburgers at a lunch counter on Main Street and tried out my new teeth on the ground maybe-chuck. It was nice being able to bite into food again. I drank a few cups of coffee, smoked a cigarette, left the joint and took a bus back to my hotel. I was staying downtown at the

Panmore and I walked through the lobby to the elevator without taking a peek at the desk. I'd been in town a week and they were about due to ask me for part of my tab, which could be embarrassing. I wasn't too flush.

In my room I found out just how flush I was. I dumped my wallet on the bed, then found the rest of my poke in the dresser between a pair of white shirts. I counted it all up and it came to a shade over eighty dollars. I owed about double that to the Panmore; I'd been eating two or three meals a day there to make my cash last as long as I could.

I put all the money in my wallet and stuck it in a pocket. I opened the top drawer of the dresser, took out a deck of cards, sat down on the bed and started to fool around with them. I ran through a couple of false shuffles, dealt a few rounds of seconds, ran cards off the bottom, practiced top-card peeks and false cuts. My left thumb was a little rusty. The boys in Chicago hadn't broken it, but they had managed to dislocate it and it took a little while to get the dexterity back. I practiced for an hour in my room and the thumb started doing what it was supposed to do.

At the end of the hour I took down the mirror from the dresser and propped it up in back of the writing desk. I sat at the desk in a straight-backed wooden chair and dealt a few rounds of seconds and bottoms while I watched myself in the mirror. When I got to the point where I couldn't even catch myself, I knew the boys at Murray Rogers' house weren't going to tip to me. It would be a profitable evening all around.

I put the mirror on the dresser, stuck the deck of cards in a drawer. I went downstairs to the bar and told the bartender to pour some Cutty Sark over some ice cubes. I sat sipping the drink and thought about Chicago and a dislocated thumb and two chipped teeth.

Chicago had been a big mistake all across the board. There are a few ways for a good card mechanic to make a living, and if that's how you make your living you have to know what those ways are. The friendly game is the easiest way—you play with solidly respectable people like Seymour Daniels and his poker buddies and you can let the deck stand up and salute without anybody tipping to the bit. The average player never looks for the gaff and never sees it when it's used on him. You don't even need to be talented—not a player in thirty can recognize a deck of marked cards if you give them to him and tell him to play solitaire with them. You can use readers all night long and nobody sees the light.

I just leveled with one approach. That's how you do it when you're on your own hook, freelancing on the poker circuit. Another is worked with a group called a card mob. There's one mechanic, a helper who crimp-cuts for him, and a few shills who do what they're supposed to do. Some amateur hookers do the steering for you, bringing the marks to the poker table as a prelude to some genital gymnastics. The marks drop their money and go home and the card mob splits the take.

In Chicago, I had tried the third way. I went into a real game against real gamblers, a table-stakes bit for heavy money. A mistake, of course, but I wanted to pick up a very fast couple of thou because there was a broad I was trying to impress and she impressed easily when you had the dough. She was a bottle-blonde with bedroom eyes and a Hollywood body. It's easy to lose your sense of balance over something like that. I lost mine. I did everything wrong.

The game had been a steady thing in the back room of an all-night drugstore. You paid five dollars an hour for your chair, and for that you had sandwiches and coffee and immunity from cops and holdup men, the latter two vocations about the same thing in Chicago. I plunged into the game cold without managing to set up a friendship with any of the players, which was a mistake right there. I sat down at ten-thirty, and by two in the morning I was twenty-three hundred dollars to the good.

Look, there's nothing easier. A fast game has a minimum of thirty hands to an hour and the game I'd been in was faster than that. The average pot held sixty or seventy bucks. The big ones held a few hundred. You don't have to win every hand to take a game for a bundle. You just have to win a little more than your share. I made sure I won enough, and I made sure I didn't always win on my deal. I palmed cards, holding out an ace or a pair until they would come in handy. I picked up the cards before my deal to leave a couple of kings sitting sixth and twelfth from the top and I made sure the shuffle didn't change the arrangement. Then a crimped card let the man to my right cut the cards right back to where I wanted them and I had kings wired to play with.

Things like that.

The hell. At two in the morning a little man with hollow eyes had seen me dealing seconds. "A goddamn number two man," he yelled. "A stinking mechanic!"

They hadn't even asked for an explanation. They took back their twenty-three hundred plus the five hundred I started with. They hauled me out behind the store and propped me up against the wall. One of them put on a pair of black leather gloves. He worked me over, putting most of his punches into my gut. The one that broke my teeth was a mistake—I slipped and fell into it, and the guy belted me in the mouth by accident. The thumb was supposed to break but only dislocated. They dragged me out to the street and gave a shove and I wound up in the gutter.

"Card mechanics die young around here," the hollow-eyed little man had said. "Maybe you shouldn't stay in Chicago too long."

And I hadn't stayed long at all. I returned to my hotel and picked up the couple of hundred bucks I'd left there in reserve. I washed up and knocked myself out with cheap liquor. The next afternoon I woke up with a hangover, dressed, packed a suitcase, skipped my bill and got the hell out of Chicago. I didn't even take time to say goodbye to my bottle-blonde—I just hopped on the first train out and left it when it hit this burg.

And for a week I didn't do anything but sleep late and drink too much and have my teeth fixed. I had the same dream every night, and each time I woke up sweating just as the men in my dream caught me cheating and stuck a gun in my face and squeezed the trigger. Each night I woke up and touched myself to make sure I was alive.

During the first few days I tried dealing now and then, trying to figure out what had gone wrong for me. The thumb didn't work at all. I hold a deck of cards in my left hand when I deal, and the left thumb is important. It has to lift the top card for peeks, and the thumb has to have just the right touch in slipping the top card out and drawing it back for second dealing. My left thumb couldn't do a thing. I gave up and got my teeth fixed and drank and dreamed bad dreams and waited it out.

The thumb was fine now. I was good enough so that Daniels and his friends wouldn't spot the cheating even if they were looking for it, and they wouldn't be looking for it. I finished my drink and ordered another, trying to figure out just how much the game would be worth to me. The average pot in the buck-limit game will hold eight or nine dollars, of which the winner puts in about two-fifty or three. That's in a five-card game; in seven-card stud the average pot runs closer to twelve, with four or five of the total coming from the winner. So you can figure the winner's profit on a hand at around six or seven dollars. If you pick up three pots more than average per hour, you'll take around a hundred dollars out of a five-hour game.

Even without giving myself the best of it, I figured to be a winner in Daniels' game. I had played the game more and I knew more about it than the rest of them. But I couldn't afford to win on talent alone. Well, change that. On talent, yes. On legit talent, no. With a little cheating the game figured to be worth two or three hundred dollars, and I figured I could win that much without their becoming suspicious.

I signed a check for my drinks and put a buck on the bar for the bartender. I caught a movie, then grabbed a meal. After dinner I took a hack to the drugstore and waited for Dentist Daniels to come to me.

Like a lamb to slaughter.

2

The big gray Olds the dentist drove was so new he hadn't got around to stripping the plastic film off the rear seats. The game was about half a mile from the drugstore he picked me up at and he chattered for the full distance, giving me a quick briefing on the game and the players. I didn't figure to need it but I let the information soak in for future reference.

There were two doctors, an insurance man, a CPA, Murray Rogers and Sy Daniels and me. Rogers and the accountant—a guy named Ed Hart—were the strong players, according to Daniels. The insurance man played a good game but gave his hands away, tightening up when he held good stuff and relaxing on a bluff. One of the doctors—either the internist or the eye man, it was hard to keep them straight—played too many hands and chased straights and flushes all night long.

I asked Daniels about his own game.

"About average," he said. "I win sometimes and I lose other times. Anything else you want to know?"

"Nothing I can think of." I laughed. "It doesn't make a hell of a lot of difference, Sy. I'll forget everything you told me the minute I sit down at the table.

That's my trouble—I get too much kick out of the game to concentrate on it."

"Well, it's no fun if you have to work too hard at it."

"That's it," I said. "When my luck runs good I win money. When it turns sour I lose. It's more a question of luck than anything else." And luck has about as much to do with poker as skill has with a crap game.

Daniels took a left turn, letting the power steering do all the work. He offered me a cigarette and I shook my head and lighted one of my own. Then he pulled the Olds over to the curb, leaned on the power brakes, parked the car. We walked a few doors down the street to an all-brick ranch set on a big lot. The grass had a fresh crew cut and the hedges were planted in toy evergreens. The doorbell played *My Dog Has Fleas* when Daniels gave it a jab. The tune was laboring through the second chorus when Murray Rogers opened the door.

"You boys are late," he rumbled. "Let's get rolling, team."

He was a big man with a heavy head and a thick neck. His hair was iron gray and he had a full mustache the same color. He was wearing gray flannel slacks and a plaid shirt open at the throat, a short-sleeved thing that let you see how muscular his arms were. He didn't look like a tax lawyer. He looked more like somebody who owned a hunting lodge, something like that.

We followed him through a built-in chrome-plated kitchen and down a flight of stairs to what they call the family room in the real estate ads. The vinyl tile on the floor was patterned to resemble parquet. The paneling was knotty cedar and the ceiling beams were exposed in mock-Colonial. Seven folding chairs crouched around an octagonal poker table, one of those functional models with wells for chips and circular spaces for drinks. Four of the chairs were occupied. The men in them stood up, Sy introduced me, and we shook hands all around.

"Sy was telling me about your accident," Murray Rogers said. "It sounded like one hell of a shakeup."

"It wasn't a picnic."

"Sounds as though you were lucky to get out of it alive."

"I was," I said. "I blew a front tire at seventy and shot off the road. I thought the car was going to flip, but it didn't. I chopped a pair of teeth on the steering wheel and caught a few body bruises. That was all."

"Lucky," the insurance man said. That was Ken Jameson.

Murray asked me what I was drinking. I said scotch would do fine. I sat down and started a fresh cigarette. Evidently Sy Daniels had filled everyone in on my cover story. I had been a plastic firm's salesman in Chicago, my job had disappeared when the company had merged with a larger outfit, and I had been heading for New York to look for work when the car had done the shimmy-shake and had wound up off the road. It was an adequate front, explaining simultaneously why I didn't have a car, why I wasn't working, and why my teeth needed a repair job.

I took the drink from Murray and sipped good scotch. Ed Hart and Harold Barnes broke open two fresh decks of Bee cards and shuffled them up. Barnes was the internist, a gangling fellow with a weak chin and thick glasses. He shuffled a final time, then ran the cards around the table until Sy caught the first jack for the deal. I bought thirty dollars worth of chips from Murray Rogers. Sy tossed his half-buck ante into the middle and we started to play. He dealt draw poker, jacks or better, and Lou Holman opened under the gun. Holman was the oculist. I caught a bust and folded before the draw. Barnes stuck around to buy one card to an open straight and picked up the pot.

I took things slow for the first half hour, laying back and getting a line on the game. It wasn't quite as friendly as Sy had made it sound. Poker never is. The object of the game is winning money, and you can only win if somebody else loses. They played a sociable sort of game but nobody was giving anything away.

I picked off a pair of baby pots in the first few rounds. Then with about twenty minutes gone I folded early in a hand of seven-card stud and held back an ace before I pitched my hand into the discard. Two hands later I caught an ace for my hole card, covering the motion by reaching for a cigarette with my free hand. I was sitting with the empty chair on my left and that made the catch a little simpler.

I bet half a buck on the ace and got three callers. On the second round I picked up a jack and Lou Holman paired his queen. He bet a buck on the queens and Ed Hart bumped a buck with a king and a five showing. I called. Barnes folded.

Everyone got garbage on the third round. Holman checked, Hart bet a buck and I raised him. Holman made a bad call—either Hart or I had to be telling the truth, and he was chasing aces or kings or both with his pair of queens. He folded on the last round and my wired aces picked up the pot when Hart called my last bet. He had kings with no help for them. I pulled in the pot.

Ken Jameson started dealing a hand of draw, and I was on his left—I raked in the cards for the shuffle. It was easy to leave three sevens on the bottom of the deck, easy to let them stay there during the shuffle. I had a bust in the draw hand but I played it anyway, wound up with just as much of a bust and folded. Then I gave the cards to Jameson for the cut.

He cut the pack. I took a cigarette, lighted it. I picked up the top half of the deck and set it back on top of the bottom, nullifying the cut. By that time Jameson didn't remember which way he cut them and nobody else was paying attention. I tossed in the ante and dealt seven-card stud, giving myself trip sevens off the bottom. On the sixth card I bought an outside pair and took the pot with sevens full over Lou Holman's flush and Sy's straight. It was a big one.

It looked like a nice evening.

I was busy losing a hand when I heard footsteps on the stairs and glanced up. I saw the legs first—long and slender, and a skirt ending at the knees. I folded my cards and had a look at the rest.

She wasn't quite beautiful. The body was perfect, with hooker's hips and queen-sized breasts and a belly that had just the right amount of bulge to it. The hair was the color of a chestnut when you pick the husk from it. She had the hair bound up in a French roll. It was stylish as hell, but you started imagining how this female was with her hair down and spread out over a white pillow.

The face was heart-shaped, with a pointed chin and wide-spaced eyes. Green eyes. There were little tension lines in the corners of those eyes, and there were matching lines around her mouth. Her mouth was a little too full and her nose was a little too long, and that's why I said she wasn't beautiful, exactly. But perfection always puts me off. There's something dry and sterile about an utterly beautiful woman. This one didn't put me off at all. She kept me staring hard at her.

"Hello, Joyce," everybody said. She gave everybody a big smile and moved across the room toward us. I glanced at Rogers. He was watching his wife with that special expression a man has when he's letting his friends survey a very desirable possession of his. She leaned over him, gave him a kiss on the side of his face. He put a hand on her hip and patted her.

"Sue just called," she said. "She'll be at the sorority house until late. She has a test of some sort she's cramming for."

"Jenny home yet?"

"She won't be home for hours, Murray. Her date's taking her to a dance and then to a party afterward." She squinted at his cards. "How are we doing?"

"So-so."

"Who's winning the money?"

"Ed's ahead," Rogers said. "And so is this son-of-a-gun Sy brought along. He plays a good game."

She regarded me. Her eyes seemed to smoke, or maybe I had too good an imagination.

"Beginner's luck," I said.

"My husband's not much for social graces," she said to me. "He hasn't introduced us yet."

Murray laughed and introduced. She gave me a funny smile, then asked if anyone would mind if she watched a few hands. No one minded. She took the empty chair at my left. Somebody shuffled the cards and started dealing. Murray gave Joyce a cigarette.

She let me light it for her, took a long drag, set the cigarette down in the ashtray. The filter tip was red from her lipstick.

She stayed for two rounds. I dealt five-card stud on my deal, took a peek at the top card after the first round was dealt. I had a five up and a king in the hole, and the top card was a king. I called the bet, then dealt seconds to the four other players and saved the king for myself. I brought an extra pair later in the hand and won a medium-sized pot.

She stubbed out her cigarette a few hands later. She stood up slowly, gracefully, walked around to Rogers and put her hand on his. Her fingers were long and slender.

"I'll come down in a few hours," she said. "I'll bring you boys something to eat."

He told her that was fine. She turned to go upstairs and the game continued while I tried to figure out how a girl who couldn't be more than thirty could have a daughter in college.

The answer wasn't that hard to dope out. It came out by itself a little later. Joyce was Rogers' second wife. The first Mrs. R. had died five or six years back and two years after that Rogers had married Joyce. He said something to the effect that she was a terrific mother to his kids, and I sat there and tried to make myself believe it. I couldn't. The hips, the eyes, the walk—she suggested a lot of things, and maternity was not among them.

But she was only another broad and Rogers was only another mark contributing to the fund for the enrichment of William Maynard. Maybe she made me hate him a little, because after she hiked up the basement stairs I thought how unfair it was that a hefty old lawyer like Rogers should have something that nice while I spent my nights alone. A deal later I punished him, did it without making a nickel for myself in the bargain. I dealt him a pat straight and gave Ken Jameson a four-card flush. Jameson didn't play cards like an insurance man. He stood heavy betting to buy a card to the flush, and I made sure I dealt him the card he needed. Murray lost heavy on that one.

She came downstairs an hour after that. It was around midnight, maybe a little after. The older daughter was home from the sorority house and she had already been downstairs to meet us and kiss Murray good night. Then Joyce appeared with a tray of sandwiches, ham and swiss on rye, and Murray took out bottles of Dutch beer from the bar refrigerator. I had a sandwich and a bottle of beer. They made a good combination.

Joyce Rogers sat in the odd chair again, relaxed in it like a cat in front of a fire. She asked who was winning and Murray laughed humorlessly.

"The rich get richer," he said, pointing at me. "And the poor get second-best hands."

"You're winning, Bill?"

"I've been getting good cards," I said.

I was up close to two hundred by then. The game figured to be good for another yard, maybe more and maybe less. I didn't want to push hard any more. It probably wouldn't be necessary. When you move out in front of a game you have a psychological edge that amounts to almost as much of an advantage as a good false shuffle. The losers tend to follow your lead and fold when you push them. Nothing succeeds like success, and nobody wins like a winner.

But you get habits. Even honest players generally manage to peek at the bottom card on the deck when they're dealing. I do it all the time, just automatically. So when I was dealing a hand and the bottom card gave me a full house, I dealt it to myself. It's a little harder coming off the bottom than it is to deal seconds, but I had been doing it all night. I filled my boat and took the pot over three fives.

"Murray," she said, "you haven't brought me flowers in the longest time."

"What brought that up?"

"Nothing," she said. "I was just thinking. I remember when I lived in New York a boy I was seeing brought met roses every day. He bought them for half a dollar from a dealer in the subway. They were the nicest roses."

Rogers laughed. "Well," he said, "the next time I'm in New York—"

"That's right," she said softly. "It would have to wait until then, wouldn't it? Because there aren't any subways in this town, and it would be impossible to find a subway dealer here."

I dropped a whole stack of chips to the floor. It was just as well, because it gave me a chance to compose myself while I hunted around and picked them up. *It would be impossible to find a subway dealer here.* Her patter was just a load of nonsense unless you happened to know the language. Then it was right on the beam.

A subway dealer is the sharp's term for a mechanic who can deal off the bottom of the deck, just as a man who can deal seconds is called a second dealer or a number-two man. So she was telling me plenty of things in a few meaningless sentences. She was saying that she had tipped to me, that she had seen the card scurry off the bottom of the deck just as cute as you please. And she was telling me that she knew the language, that she knew things about poker that you couldn't find in Yardley's book on the subject.

But she wasn't telling tales. She was playing little games with me, sitting there at my left and watching me take her husband's money away from him without a whisper. She wouldn't dream of mentioning it to him. And she wouldn't dream of letting me think she didn't know about it. She had to put a small bug in my ear just to keep her hand in.

We broke at two-thirty. I cashed in three hundred ten dollars worth of chips and wound up a cool two hundred eighty dollars to the good. Ed Hart was up thirty or forty dollars. The other five men went for sixty to seventy bucks apiece. It was a hard hit but nothing harder than any of them could afford.

"Back next week, Bill?"

"I don't know," I said. "I suppose I'll be long gone by then. Now that Sy's put my teeth back together, I ought to get on down to New York and see about setting up some job interviews."

"Be a shame to lose you," Lou Holman said. "We ought to get a chance at taking our money back."

"This isn't a bad place to live," Rogers said. "It's a good size for a city, big enough to be interesting and small enough to be fairly friendly. You don't have any ties anywhere, do you?"

"None."

"Never married?"

"Once," I said. "It didn't work out." Which was true enough, and which was something I rarely talked about. Or thought about if I could avoid it.

"You could probably make a good connection here," Rogers resumed. "New York's a fairly cold place, despite the florists my wife seems to be nostalgic about. There are some plastics outfits here—I don't know much about them, but there's probably somebody around who could use a good man."

"Don't talk him into it," Harold Barnes said. "It'll cost us money to keep him in town. He plays too strong a game."

"Hell," Murray said, "I just want a chance to get it back."

We had a laugh or two over that. I put my winnings in my wallet and Murray showed us to the door. Sy Daniels insisted on giving me a ride to the Panmore and I didn't argue all that hard. He wanted to talk about poker but I switched the conversation around to Mrs. Murray Rogers. He drove through empty streets with a smelly cigarette in his mouth and he talked about her.

"She's a lot of woman," he said. "That's not hard to see, is it?"

I muttered something noncommittal.

"I'll tell you," he said. "To be perfectly frank, I thought Murray was being a damned fool when he married her. He's around fifty, you know, and she's almost twenty years younger than he is. That's a lot of distance. When a middle-aged man falls for a younger woman he can wind up looking like a jackass. Especially when the woman looks like Joyce does."

"But it's working for him?"

Sy grinned. "He looks happy, doesn't he? We all figured she was marrying him for his dough. He's got a lot of it, Bill. A good tax man writes his own ticket these days and Murray is damned good. But you can't ask for more devotion than that girl has shown him. She cooks for him, she doesn't work overtime spending his money, she doesn't play around. And she's a pretty sweet girl. He was right and we were wrong, Bill. He got a good deal."

At the hotel Sy asked me himself if there were any chance I would stay in town for a while. I told him I didn't honestly know one way or the other. If he had asked me that afternoon, I would have told him I'd be on the first plane to New York in the morning. But that was a long time ago.

I shook hands with him, thanked him for the game and for the ride. Once in my room, I counted my money, putting aside two yards in my hiding place in the dresser.

Then I undressed and stood under the shower, letting a stream of hot water soak some of the tension out of my body.

A long poker session exhausts anyone. If you play worth a damn you have your mind on every player, throughout every hand, and you wind up sitting in one position on a not-all-that-comfortable chair until your rear end aches just as much as your head does.

If you're a mechanic, you wind up twice as exhausted. You don't just have to play your cards. You have to make sure you obtain winning cards, and you have to watch out every second that nobody sees what you're doing. I was dead and my nerves were on edge.

The shower helped and, when I was finished with it, the bed had never seemed more comfortable.

Of, course I didn't fall asleep right away. I lay under the covers in the dark room and listened to occasional traffic noises outside my window. And I thought about something lovely, something with green eyes and chestnut hair and a body that looked warm, inviting.

A pretty sweet girl—Sy Daniels had called her that. Also a girl who could spot a damned smooth bottom deal and identify it in card sharp's code. Who the hell was she? What angle was she working?

I tossed the questions back and forth and made everything but answers. Then the questions faded slowly to black and I fell asleep.

3

Again, the same dream. This time there was a slight variation—I was dealing poker in the same Chicago backroom, there were six of us around a green, felt-topped table, a shaded light bulb hung some eighteen inches above the center of the table, and the room was thick with smoke. I dealt five-card stud. I gave cards to the players—ace of clubs, ace of hearts, ace of diamonds, ace of clubs, ace of hearts, ace of diamonds. Everyone was staring at me, eyes angry. I took the pack and riffled through it, and every card in the pack was the ace of spades, the death card. Someone drew a knife, and someone else drew a gun, and I ran through cold dark streets with half the world chasing me—

The telephone eventually woke me. Before it did, though, I tried to weave the ringing into the pattern of the dream. The telephone kept on ringing until I came up for air and sat up in bed. I was sweating, and I couldn't manage to catch my breath as I picked up the instrument.

"Hello?" I said.

Soft laughter, first. Then: "Did I wake you, Bill?"

"Oh," I said.

"It's me. Weren't you expecting me?"

"I suppose I was."

"You're a good subway dealer, Bill. How did you wind up last night?"

"Ahead."

She laughed again. "I want to see you," she said.

"Where are you?"

"A block from your hotel. Can I come up?"

I took a breath. "Give me ten or fifteen minutes," I said. "I'm not awake yet."

I hung up, rubbed my eyes, moved out of bed. My cigarettes were on the dresser. I smoked a butt part way and stubbed it out in the ashtray. Then I picked up the phone and told room service what to send up for breakfast. I grabbed a fast shave, washed up, dressed. I put on a tie and a tweed jacket and tried combing a certain amount of order into my hair.

The doorbell rang. A waiter brought in a tray loaded down with orange juice, corned beef hash, toast and coffee. I signed the tab and slipped him a buck. I was finished with the food and working on the coffee when the phone rang and somebody told me that a Mrs. Rogers was there to see me. I told the voice to send her up.

I finished the coffee, started a cigarette. There was a knock at the door. I opened it and the room became perceptibly warmer.

Joyce wore a tan sweater and a dark brown skirt. Her green eyes were hard and soft at once—emeralds one moment and card-table felt the next. She drew the door shut behind her, then stepped past me and crossed the room to the bed. She sat on it, tucking a long leg beneath herself, while I wished I had taken the time to make up the bed. But she didn't seem to mind. She had a lot of class, and yet you got the impression she was accustomed to unmade beds.

"You look puzzled," she said.

"I am."

"Why?"

"Because I don't know who you are," I said. "You're supposed to be Murray Rogers' devoted wife, young and lovely and sweet. You sat down at the table last night and watched a few hands and spotted some of the smoothest card manipulation anybody's likely to see anywhere. You called me on it in gambler's argot without letting anybody know you tipped to me. And you let me take close to three yards out of the game without saying a word. I don't get it."

She opened her purse, withdrew a flat silver case. She took out a cork-tipped cigarette and put it between her red lips. Just sitting there, she managed to give off more sexuality than a stripper in Baltimore. I struck a match to give her a light and she took hold of my wrist to steady the flame. Her fingers pressed harder than they had to and her eyes held mine. Something happened, with electricity in it. I couldn't look away from her.

Joyce said, "Who do you think I am, Bill?"

"I'd like to know."

"Take a guess."

I crossed to the dresser and stared at her reflection in the mirror. They say every man has a weakness. They say that for every man there's a woman somewhere in the world who can make him jump through fiery hoops just by snapping her fingers. They say a man's lucky if he never meets that woman.

All of a sudden I knew what they meant.

"Bill?"

"I think you used to sleep with a gambler," I said.

"I used to sleep with lots of men."

"Maybe." I turned to face her. "You got out of it. You latched on to Rogers and married him. Evidently you've been playing it straight since then. Last night you watched me cheat and didn't say a word. You could have queered things. You didn't."

"Honor among thieves?" she said.

"More."

"What?"

"You could have just ignored me. You didn't have to let on that you saw the bottom deal. You sure as hell didn't have to come here today. You want something."

"Oh? What do I want, Bill?"

"You tell me."

Joyce didn't answer with words. Instead, she stood up, that perfect body unfolding gracefully from the bed. I watched her while she tugged the tan sweater free from the waistband of her skirt, then pulled the sweater over her head and tossed the knit aside. My mouth became dry and my throat knotted up. She took off her skirt and her bra and her slip, her stockings and her panties. She did a sweet little strip and wound up standing there by the side of my bed, bare as the truth, and she smiled like an oversexed version of the Mona Lisa.

With clothes on she had been almost beautiful. Now, nude, she was a goddess. The tips of her flawless breasts were stiff with preliminary passion. Her hips flared in an obscene invitation to Paradise. Her eyes were all fog and smoke.

"What do I want, Bill?"

Joyce walked toward me. Gears locked within me. I didn't move toward her or away from her. I stood very still and she came closer. Her breasts jutted out like mortar shells. I could smell her perfume mingling with the hot animal scent of her body. She came closer, and I felt her body heat, and her lips were inches from mine. If I raised her face or lowered mine I could have kissed her. I didn't.

"Bill—"

Then I did.

At first our lips just touched. Then a few bombs exploded and a few bells rang and all bets were off. I crushed her close, felt her breasts press hard against my chest, tasted her bittersweet mouth. Her arms were about me and I felt her and smelled her and tasted her and ached for her. My hands moved over her flesh. She was soft and sweet and warm.

Somehow I slipped out of my clothes. Somehow we steered ourselves to the bed where I filled my hands with the bounty of her breasts and she made little animal sounds from somewhere deep in her throat. I kissed her and her nails dug into my shoulders and the world took off on a joyride.

I ran my hands all over Joyce's body like a skeptic searching for a flaw. No flaws, just perfection. I touched her legs, her thighs. I brushed my face over her flat stomach and she took my head in her arms and cradled it between her breasts.

Her voice was far away, husky, deep. "What do you think I want, Bill?"

We answered the question in the unmade bed with the lights on and the shades up. The room was on a high floor, so no one could have seen us, but we never thought about that at the time one way or the other. The lovemaking was too fast, too furious, too compulsive. There was deep need and dark hunger, and flesh merging with flesh, and an orchestral swell out of Tschaikovsky that led to a coda of pure Stravinsky.

That vital dissonance was always there. That harsh and bitter beauty that tossed the conventional harmonies out the window...

*

The world took a long time coming back together again. Joyce lay back and smoked a cigarette. I curled up beside her warmth and took the pins from her hair. She smiled like a cat while I took down her hair and spread it out over the pillow. Fresh chestnuts on new snow.

"How did you start, Bill?"

"You started. You called me up and—"

"No. How did you start cheating at cards?"

I hadn't told the story in a long time. When you live your life according to a certain pattern and when you fit part and parcel into a certain world, it's hard to remember another living pattern and the other world you used to inhabit. When one world is law-abiding and the other is the gray world of the card mechanic, the two spheres are especially far apart. I remembered the first world, of course, but I seldom thought much about it.

Well, I hadn't told the story in a long time, and Joyce had asked, so I felt talkative. I told her the story of a young guy named Maynard the Magnificent who had done magic tricks. Sleight-of-hand with cards and matchboxes and silk scarves. A batch of pretty decent bits tied together with some easy patter and a certain amount of stage presence. Add some mentalist routines, toss in the white tie and the tails and a supposedly debonair moustache, and you had Maynard.

I had never been big. For one thing, I hadn't been that good. For another, there aren't a hell of a lot of big magicians around. Can you name four magicians offhand? And don't name Thurston or Houdini or Blackstone, because they were all a long time ago. They played vaudeville houses then and they were big draws. A magician isn't a big draw nowadays. He's something to fill up the card at a burlesque house, something only slightly more amusing than the shopworn blackout bits. He's an added unattraction in Miami Beach hotels and borscht belt resorts. He's something they pay twenty-five bucks to for entertaining a batch of snotty kids at a ten-year-old's birthday party.

Maynard the Magnificent. I had had to fight like hell to snag lousy billings, and it was a nothing road to nowhere. From time to time I thought of junking magic and finding a job in a widget factory. This never happened. For one thing, I didn't know or care very much about widgets. For another, I was still a young guy who pulled a kick out of magic tricks. I didn't need the big money or the comfy security.

Then there had been a girl named Carole—the woman I sawed in half, the girl who brought out the wagon of props and enchanted the audience with her mammary development. She was fifth in the series of my assistants. They come and they go. This one stayed awhile; she was prettier than the others and warmer than the others and I was twenty-eight instead of twenty-two. I taught her special tricks at night and we made special magic in dark rooms, and we wound up standing in front of a justice of the peace to make it all legal.

There had been a big change. Two can't live as cheaply as one. Two can't live as cheaply as one plus one, either. The whole is monetarily greater than the sum of its parts. Two can't go too far on apple pie and coffee in roadside diners and one-night stands in sleazy resorts.

But it had been good at first. It became a little less than good, then worse, until there was that night at a waterfront motel in Miami when a dark-eyed man approached me after I'd finished entertaining my captive audience.

"Wizard," he said, "I want to talk to you."

I told him to go ahead.

"Someplace private. I got a car outside, Wizard."

So I told Carole to wait for me, and I accompanied the dark-eyed man to his car. It was that year's Caddy, long and black. He sat behind the wheel and I sat next to him. He gunned the car north on Collins Avenue, made small talk while we passed through Golden Beach where the millionaires live in oceanfront mansions. He gave me a cigarette, took one for himself, and started talking through smoke.

"Wizard," he said, "how much money do you make?"

"Not much."

"You got a valuable talent," he said. "You need training, but you got a valuable talent."

"If you're trying to sell me correspondence courses—"

He laughed. "Wizard," he said, "you ever play any cards?"

Thurston once said he never played cards—if he won they would accuse him of cheating, if he lost they would say he was a lousy magician. I had never played much. The dark-eyed man talked about cards, and about what you could do if your fingers were clever. Then he talked about money. I told him I would have to think things over. He drove me back to the motel—Carole and I had a room there during the engagement and he gave me a card. His name, his phone number. Nothing else.

The next day I called my agent. The motel gig was due to end on Saturday and he didn't have us booked for anything until the following Thursday. I put the phone on the hook and asked Carole if she felt like going for a swim. She whined something to the effect that she couldn't wear the same damn bathing suit day in and day out. I told her to buy a new one. She said a decent bathing suit cost twenty bucks minimum and we couldn't afford it.

That night I called the dark-eyed man. A girl answered. He took the phone from her and asked who I was.

"Bill Maynard," I said. "Maynard the Magnificent."

"What do you say, Wizard?"

I said, "I'll play."

We played ten hours a day for the next two weeks. We played in a suite at a hotel. There was the dark-eyed man, a heavy type named Guiterno who was bankrolling the operation, a long-fingered Cuban and a nervous little blond girl. They taught me how to play straight and crooked, showed me the moves for false-dealing and palming, taught me to hold the deck in the mechanic's grip with the index finger in front and the other three fingers around the side of the deck, thumb poised to do little tricks. They taught me gin rummy and poker and blackjack and pinochle and by the time they were finished I was good enough to roll.

The start was in a solarium on top of a big strip hotel. There was a character from New York, a paunchy bastard who came down to the beach twice a year for three weeks to sit in the sun, and screw call girls and play gin rummy. We played for two dollars a point. In three days I had eight thousand dollars of his money. Sixty-five hundred went to my trainer and I was fifteen hundred to the good.

That had been just the start.

Carole hadn't known about it at first. Somewhere along the line she found out, and somewhere further along the line she left. Whatever it was we'd had, it didn't work in the new world I'd managed to find for myself. Somewhere along the line the mob split. I found a partner and played ocean-liner bridge on the *Queen Mary*. We sailed to Le Havre and back and let the opposition pay for the trip. Somewhere along the line I soloed. And somewhere along the line, in Chicago, I hung myself up on a bottle-blonde and looked to pick the wrong kind of people. They caught me and broke my teeth and dislocated my thumb and told me to get the hell out of town…

4

Outside, something was heading north on Main Street with its siren open. It was either a police cruiser or an ambulance, I couldn't tell which, but it was making a hell of a lot of noise. I crossed to the window and stood there straightening my tie and trying to see what it was. But it had passed out of view by then.

I turned to Joyce. She was dressed now, and she was trying to manage that chestnut hair back into its French roll. I walked up behind her and kissed the back of her neck. She spun around and put her hands against my chest.

"I suppose only a dentist like Seymour Daniels would look a gift horse in the mouth," I said.

"What's that supposed to mean?"

"It means I'm a dentist at heart. I still want to know why you came here this morning."

"Because I missed you, Bill."

I gave her a funny look. She finished playing with her hair, took a cigarette, lighted it. "I missed you," she said again. "Oh, not you in particular. Men like you. People like you. I've been married to Murray for almost three years and I'm still not used to it. Life had more of a kick to it before. I didn't spend it cooking meals and entertaining business friends and going to dances at the country club. I stayed up late and slept late and lived hard. I was hungry all the time. Hungry for people, hungry for things to do. That's what I missed."

"Don't you like what you've got?"

"No."

"It must be a hell of a lot easier," I said. "No worries about money or law. Good whiskey to drink and expensive clothes to wear."

"I had that before."

"All the time?"

"No. Some of the time." Joyce looked at her feet. "Listen, of course it's easier. That's not everything, Bill. Dying is the easiest thing in the world, just lying down and dying and never having to hustle again. And being married to Murray Rogers is a lot like dying. The kick is gone. There's no motion, no excitement."

Maybe I'd been too close to broke to feel sorry for anybody with a world full of money. Whatever it was, it must have showed on my face. She saw it.

"Bill, you could have stayed hooked up with a card mob. It's safer that way, isn't it?"

"Sure."

"Why didn't you?"

"I didn't like to work for somebody else," I said. "I wanted it a little freer than that. Hell, when I dealt for Guiterno I was just a well-paid hired hand."

"Now do you understand?"

I nodded. "Cheer up," I said. "He's not a kid any more. He's around fifty and he's worked hard all his life. He's a good twenty years older than you are. He won't live forever. You'll be a young widow with a pot full of dough and a lifetime to spend it in."

And then she was laughing. It was loose, hysterical laughter. She threw back her head and her whole body shook with the laughter, and she kept going until I grabbed her by the shoulders and calmed her down. Then she looked straight in my eyes and started to laugh again.

"So funny," she said. "So very funny."

"What is?"

"Everything. That's what everybody thinks—I'll stick it out and I'll be a rich young widow and everything will be great. That's what I thought, Bill. Murray let me think so. I should have made him put it in writing, damn it."

I didn't reach it.

"He's richer than God," she said. "He's also a lawyer, and he's got a very pretty little will drawn up. One hundred thousand dollars goes in trust for me. I get the income from it until I remarry or move out of town. If I do either, the trust is dissolved and the principal is divided between those two rich-bitch daughters of his. They also get the rest of the estate over and above the hundred thousand, and that comes to so much that they wouldn't even miss that hundred thou. I get the house, too—but I don't get to own it outright. The trust owns it. I live in it rent-free. If I remarry or move away from this city, I lose the house along with the money."

"So you don't get a thing?"

"Nothing. Maybe five or six thousand dollars income from the trust, if I want to spend my life rotting. Oh, something else, and you'll love this part. If I'm still unmarried and living here on my fiftieth birthday, then I get the principal of the trust, the whole happy little pie. But by then I'll be too old to do anything with it. Isn't that cute, Bill?"

It was cute, all right. Joyce had married him for a soft touch, and he had fixed it so that the soft touch ended the day he died. I asked her what would happen if she divorced him.

"Divorce a lawyer?" She shook her head. "That's like fighting city hall, Bill. I wouldn't get a nickel. No, there are only two things I can do. I can leave him flat and go back to the old life without taking any of his money along. Or I can keep it up the way it is and hope he lives forever. The will's unbreakable, of course. He knows how to make a will unbreakable."

She checked her make-up in the mirror, seemed happy with what she saw. She turned to me and gave me a kiss, and I caught her in my arms and messed up her lipstick all over again. Her arms held on tight.

"Damn it," she said.

"You could come with me, Joyce."

"And live on what?"

"Other people's money, for a starter."

"Why not Murray's money?"

"Let him keep it."

"I gave him almost three years," she said. "Do I write them off now? Throw it up and say to hell with three years? You don't get that many years, Bill. You have to hold onto them, make them swing for you. I don't want to throw three of them away."

"It's worse to throw them all away."

She was clinging to me and her face was pressed against my throat. She sagged, and I held onto her to keep her from crumbling. Then I felt her chest swell as she gulped in air. Her breasts were tight against me. I let go of her and she straightened up.

"I started to fall apart," Joyce said.

"Forget it. You're all right now."

"I'd like to stick with you. Live with you, travel with you. You're my kind of people, Bill."

I didn't say anything.

"But I like his money. I have a big thing for his money. Wouldn't it be nice if we could find a way to put the two together?"

She let that one hang in the air for a few seconds. Then her face changed and she gave me a fast smile. She did a patchwork job on her lipstick, tossed her purse over her arm.

"I've got to run," she told me. "I'm supposed to be downtown on a minor shopping spree. I'll have to duck into a department store and buy a few sweaters in a hurry, then get back to our little ranch-style castle. Will you be staying in town for a while, Bill?"

"I suppose so. I don't have any place to go."

"I thought you were going to New York."

"So did I."

She looked at me, and her lips parted in a pout a little subtler than the Marilyn Monroe pose, but not much. "Then we'll be seeing each other," she said. "Goodbye, Wizard."

After she left, I took the elevator down and let the hotel barber shorten my hair. When he was finished, I was a little less shaggy and a little more ex-Ivy League. I stopped at the desk on the way through the lobby and picked up my bill. The room clerk took my money and said something pleasant when I told him I'd be sticking around for awhile. I left the hotel and took a walk along Main Street.

Wouldn't it be nice if we could find a way to put the two together? Not two, though. Three. Joyce and the money and me. We three, we're not a crowd. We're just a starry dream.

There was a classic answer to the classic problem. The problem read Boy meets Girl, Girl has Rich Husband, and the answer read, Boy kills Husband,

Boy gets Girl and Money. But we didn't fit the classic problem. If we killed Murray we didn't win anything but the electric chair. If he died, there was no money for the weeping widow.

It was just as well. The heavy-handed touch is not exactly the hallmark of the card mechanic. The brute type doesn't bother slipping a deck of readers into the game or filling a flush from the bottom of the deck. The brute type takes his mark into a handy alleyway and hits him on the head with something heavy.

A mechanic is just a con man. He cons with a deck the way another man cons with a pool cue or a pair of wrong-way dice or a portfolio of Canadian moose-pasture stocks. And a con man plays the game with certain rules operating inside of his head. The direct approach is not on the preferred list.

Sometimes matters are ridiculous. When I had been dealing for Guiterno, we had a game set up for a Texan who liked to play big-money blackjack. That's a dealer's-control game—if you can deal seconds, and if you use marked cards or know how to do top-card peeks, you can make your mark lose every hand. A wide-hipped hooker steered the Texan to our game and he was the only live one in the crew. I was dealing and there were four of five shills playing with Guiterno's money. It was all set up for the Texan.

And the Texan had been stoned to the gills on charcoal-filtered bourbon. He moved into the room where the game was floating, plumped himself down in the seat we had carefully kept open for him, and slapped a wad of long green on the table. He was so blind he couldn't see the spots on the cards. He didn't know where he was or what he was doing there, and we could have pocketed his money and put him out to pasture in the middle of the street without worrying about any mess in the morning. He wouldn't remember a thing.

But we took his roll one hand at a time, and we kept playing hand after goddamned hand until fifty-four yards of his money had made the pilgrimage from his side of the table to our side. I even dealt hands to the shills, and the shills played out the hands religiously, and we took that Texan's money just the way it says in the book, hand by hand and bet by bet. A few times he bet a hundred dollars on a card and lost and paid off with two bills stuck together. And I very honestly separated the bills and gave one back to him so that he could lose it on the next round.

We had cleaned the Texan according to the con man's code, such as it is.

So it was just as well that Murray Rogers wouldn't solve our problems by dying, or by being killed. Because I wasn't trained for that kind of action.

I smoked a few cigarettes, stopped at a few diners and lunch counters for coffee. I thought about packing a suitcase and catching the plane to New York, but I didn't think very seriously. I knew damned well I wasn't going to do it, and I knew why.

Joyce Rogers hadn't come to my room for a quick tumble and a chorus of *Auld Lang Syne.* And I wasn't staying in town for another grab at her sweet brass ring or another poker session with Murray and Sy and the boys. We were both looking for an angle, the same angle. An angle that would give Maynard the Magnificent a pile of money and a green-eyed girl with hair the color of chestnuts.

The angle had to be there. All I had to do was find it.

5

I returned to the hotel in time to pick up a message from Sy Daniels. The terse little slip said I was supposed to call him. I put the call through from my room and reached him at his office. He wanted me to have dinner over at his place. It didn't especially appeal but I seemed to be locked into it; I couldn't very well turn him down two days running. I accepted the invitation with a certain amount of enthusiasm and he told me to drop over to the office around five-thirty and he'd give me a lift.

"Never mind," I told him. "I rented a car a few hours ago. I may be in town a few days and I'd just as soon be able to drive myself around."

I took down the address he gave me and the instructions on finding the place. I tucked this valuable information away in my wallet and found the Hertz outfit. A tired old man with cigarette-stained fingers took a long look at my driver's license and condescended to rent me a car.

I asked for a stick shift. He had a hard time getting it through his head that I didn't want automatic transmission and kept telling me that Hertz paid for the gas anyway. I told him I liked to feel as though I were doing the driving. Finally he gave me the car I wanted and wrote me off as an enemy of progress. I took the car out and drove it around to get the feel of it. It was a piece of tin with nothing much in the engine department, but I didn't feel much like a Gran Prix contender myself. I just drove.

Half of my mind worried about the driving. The other half fooled around with a green-eyed girl and her rich husband. Renting the car had been a commitment, if one were needed. I wasn't going to catch a plane to New York, I was going to stick around, me and my tinny rental, and something was going to happen.

We couldn't kill him. He had to be alive, and he had to have the money taken away from him. Well, I'd been taking money away from men for years. But I wasn't going to beat Murray Rogers for a few hundred thou with a deck of cards. When a man worth somewhere around a million can pick a kick out of buck-limit poker, he doesn't exactly fit the high-roller class. So my talent as a mechanic wasn't going to be all that helpful.

There were a few possibles. Murray Rogers could flip his lid and be committed to a funny farm. That would leave him alive and keep his loaded will from going into effect, and it would heap the money in Joyce's warm little hands. If he went nuts, in short, she could divorce him without any trouble and obtain the kind of settlement that would let us sit pretty—maybe half to her and half to him for the girls, or something along those lines. Or, she could just find a way to divert the dough from her pocket to ours. That would be easy with him out of the way for awhile.

Two ways, then. A con that would strip the dough from Murray or would hit a way to ease him out of town long enough for Joyce and I to obtain control of the money. It was comforting to figure it all out that way, but that was about all. The chance of Murray going insane spontaneously was remote enough, and the chance that we could drive him nuts was just as far-fetched.

The traffic became progressively thicker, and by the time it was jammed up tight it was time to head for dinner with Daniels. My car swam through traffic like a salmon heading upstream. I followed Daniels' directions without being lost more than once, and I parked in front of his house at a quarter after six.

Dinner wasn't bad. Sy Daniels had a wife who was evidently trying to buck Joyce in the youth department. And failing, not surprisingly. Mary Daniels dyed her gray hair back to what she wished were its original color, and the ash-blonde result didn't fit her complexion at all. Her eyes were older than the rest of her face and her girdle faded in the two-way stretch. But she kept a nice home and cooked a good meal and hadn't picked up the annoying habit of flirting with her husband's friends, which was nice. We ate brisket and roasted potatoes and asparagus tips, and afterward we sat around in the living room and drank scotch on the rocks.

The conversation roamed around, but it took on a definite tone in the course of the evening. Sy asked me if I were looking for work. I told him I'd gone as far as probing the classifieds with a pencil and checking off things that looked remotely possible. Later Mary wanted to know how I liked the town. Sy said something about how a man needed to put down roots after a certain amount of rambling around. Mary dragged some broad into the conversation and hinted that she could fix me up if I were interested.

It was all as homey as a Norman Rockwell cover, and I was the only one who knew what was wrong with this picture. They had life all planned for me. I would pick up a good job—there was a hint to the effect that one of Sy's friends could probably come up with something if I decided to get off the plastics merry-go-round—and I would meet a nice girl who was hubby-hunting, and I would buy a house in the suburbs and play poker every Friday night and join the country club and fish for bass at the lake and otherwise spin in their social circle.

All in all, it wasn't an illogical notion on their part.

From their point of view the notion was perfectly feasible and desirable. But what they didn't know was that I was staying in town because I was hung on somebody's wife. This would have jarred them. My thing with Joyce killed their rose-covered dream for me. And if I broke it off with Joyce and folded the hand I'd be out of town like a shot.

And, to carry it a little further, if Joyce and I found a way to keep Murray Rogers alive but irrelevant, and if I won the girl and the money, girl and I would have no particular use for Sy and Mary and they would have less use for us. So there was quite a bit wrong with Rockwell's cover. But the scotch was good and the company was pleasant and I stayed there until nearly midnight. Then I drove the Corvair back to the hotel, let the doorman put it to bed, and rode upstairs to do the same for myself. It took a good hour before I fell asleep. My mind kept taking things and turning them over and over, making up fresh problems and looking for answers that didn't seem to be there.

I slept, finally. I had a bad dream, but in the morning I couldn't remember what it was about.

I called her a little before noon. The voice that answered didn't sound like hers. It was younger, softer.

I said, "Mrs. Rogers?"

The voice said, "Just a minute." Then there was an offstage, "Joyce! Telephone!"

A few seconds later another voice said "Hello," and this time it was the right one.

"You sound lovely this morning," I said. "Who was I talking to before?"

"Oh, good morning, Mr. Hewlitt," she said. "I wanted to talk to you about my monthly statement. It came this morning."

"There's somebody in the room with you."

"Yes," she said. "That's right."

"Can you get away this afternoon?"

"I really don't think so, Mr. Hewlitt."

"Tonight?"

"Well, that's possible, I suppose."

"Name a time."

"There's a charge for eight dollars and thirty cents here that I really don't understand."

"Eight-thirty tonight?"

"Yes, that's right."

"Where?"

"Well, I'm not sure exactly. I can't say, Mr. Hewlitt."

"You want me to pick a place?"

"That's right."

"My hotel?"

A pause. Then: "I should think there would be a better way than that to handle the matter."

I thought for a minute. "There's a bar at Main and Utica," I said. "Southwest corner. I'll be there at eight-thirty. Drive by and give a honk."

"Fine," she said. "I'd appreciate that."

"I wish you were here now, Joyce. I'd like to rip your clothes off and pitch you onto a bed."

"Yes," she said, calmly, levelly. "Yes, of course. Certainly."

I spent the afternoon in a movie. It was a Sunday, so Rogers was probably home, and that no doubt explained why she couldn't get away during the afternoon. The monthly statement routine had sounded a little less than brilliant to me—not too many credit managers make adjustments on Sunday morning. But that was Joyce's problem. I had the feeling that there wasn't anybody in the room with her anyway, that she was just exercising a talent for melodrama.

The movie was dull. I walked out somewhere in the middle of the last reel and went across the street to a lunch counter. I had a hot pastrami sandwich on rye and a cup of black coffee. The check came to eighty-five cents or so. I left a quarter on the counter for the waitress, then carried my check to the cashier. I gave her a ten and she handed me my change.

The rest was almost reflex. My fingers tucked the five down and held it so that it stayed out of sight while my palm was up. It all happened in one quick movement while I was reaching with my other hand for a toothpick. Then I picked through my change and told the frayed blond cashier that she had made a mistake—

I had given her a ten and she was five bucks short. She stared at the bills and coins in my hand, then at the fresh ten on the register. She shrugged her bony shoulders in puzzlement and gave me another five. I stuffed everything in a handy pocket and stepped outside.

Cheap, I thought. Cheap and shabby. I walked back to the hotel and picked up the car and tried on the way to figure out why I'd picked the girl for an extra five dollars. I didn't need the money. Maybe my action had been force of habit. Maybe I had been showing off to myself, proving how much faster the trained hand is than the untrained eye.

I left the car on the avenue and found the bar where I was supposed to wait for Joyce. It was a block from Daniels' office and I'd had a drink or two there one day after a particularly bad session of drilling and grinding. That had been in the afternoon. Now it was early evening and the place was worse than I remembered it. There were a few embryonic derelicts drinking cheap wine and a few young punks getting high from the smell of the beers in front of them. I ordered a bottle of beer and got a cigarette started.

At eight o'clock I started watching the street. I watched for the full half hour. Then a Caddy convertible pulled up at the curb and she hit the horn, right on schedule. I scooped my change from the bar top and left half my beer as a tip. I figured it would be served up as a glass of draft in that kind of saloon.

The Caddy's door was open. I hopped in, yanked the door shut. She drove a block, made an illegal U-turn and headed uptown.

"I ought to have a trenchcoat," she said. "I feel like something out of a movie."

"A bad movie."

"A vehicle for a shining young starlet," she said. Her hand left the wheel and went to her hair. "You could tell me how beautiful I look, Wizard."

"I thought I was Mr. Hewlitt."

She laughed easily. "Sue was in the room. She was the one who answered the phone."

"The one who calls you Joyce?"

"She couldn't call me mother. I'm a hot ten years older than she is. The little bitch hates me, Bill. I'm cast as the wicked stepmother in her little playlet. Jennie isn't so bad. She's the younger one. She thinks I'm wonderful because I'm pretty and I dress well and I have bigger breasts than she does."

"That last doesn't surprise me."

"Is that as close as you can come to a compliment?"

I told her I'd do better when we turned into a motel. She said we weren't going to a motel, Murray was home, she only had an hour or so. I asked her where we were going and she said something about a gin mill where we wouldn't run into anybody she knew. We stayed with Main Street, turned after a mile or two, and wound up at a little neighborhood tavern just inside the city line. A bar, a television set, a jukebox, three booths. We took the last booth. The juke was unplugged and the television set was tuned to Ed Sullivan. The bartender was watching the show. There were two beer-drinkers in the place and that was all.

The bartender glanced our way. I asked for Cutty Sark on the rocks for both of us. He didn't have any. I tried him on Vat 69 and Peter Dawson and he didn't have those fellows either. We settled on Black and White. He brought it over and Joyce and I touched glasses and drank. Most of her scotch disappeared on the first swallow. She shivered a little, then let out a sigh. I asked what was wrong.

"Nothing," she said. "Or everything. I don't know. Why did you have to come to this city, Wizard?"

"I blew a tire and went off the road."

"We all went off the road," she said. "Ages ago. I couldn't sit still after I spoke to you on the phone. I was all jumpy and nervous, and then Murray got home from some committee meeting out at the club, and I had to sit around, make small talk and let him pat my behind and kiss my neck and put his big hands on me. I never minded it that much before. I could turn myself off, and now and then I could sell myself on the idea that we were in some kind of love."

She finished the rest of her drink and made rings on the table with her empty glass. I lit two cigarettes and gave her one. Her fingers brushed my hand as she took the cigarette and it happened again just as it had happened in my room at the Panmore. This was not somebody else's wife sitting across the table from me. This was a woman.

"Bill, I've done some rotten things—"

"To hell with that."

"Let me finish. I've done rotten things. I've been around. I've been all over the map. But I can't lay two men at the same time, one for love and one for money. I don't groove that way. I couldn't wait to get out of that house tonight. I can't stand the idea of going back to it."

"Then don't."

"Uh-huh," she said.

"Don't," I said. "We'll take the car and go away. We won't come back."

Her eyes were on the empty glass. Not empty; ice cubes were busy melting in it. She didn't say anything for a few minutes and when she spoke her voice was low and hard.

"For two months," she said. "Maybe three. Until we hit a hard time and I remember how easy it was to do nothing and live high. We couldn't make it without money, Wizard."

After a few more minutes I took our glasses to the bartender and he filled them up again. I brought them back and we drank. She asked me if I'd managed to work up any ideas. I told her that Murray could go insane or skip the country or get himself conned for a fortune.

"We'd go insane before he did," she said.

"Probably."

"I was thinking," she said. "We could kidnap me. I could disappear and you could call him on the phone and tell him to get a hundred grand in small bills and leave it somewhere. He would pay, Bill. And then we could go like the wind."

"A fake kidnapping?"

"Why not? I would whimper into the phone and say how they were going to rape me and kill me and everything. What's wrong with it?"

"A lot of things. The money would be marked, it's always marked in kidnap deals. There are people who buy marked money for something like thirty or forty cents on the dollar, more or less depending how hot it is. And it would be hotter than hell on this deal because when you didn't turn up they'd figure you were dead. Even if he didn't go to the cops right away, he'd go to them afterward. With the FBI in the picture we wouldn't stand a chance."

"I could go back to him after the payoff. Then I could leave him later."

"I still don't like it," I said. "Too many things can go wrong. With all those variables to play with, one thing's sure to turn sour and ruin the whole game. Picking up the money is hard enough with a whole mob in the show. It's tougher than hell to work two-handed."

"It was an idea."

"A cute one. But it won't play."

She worked on her drink. I stared down at the table and told myself it was time to skip. There was no way to have the girl and the money, and the girl wouldn't come along unless the money came too. This wasn't my type of scene. In the morning I could be on my way, headed for New York and a world I knew.

Then I lifted my eyes and threw the thought away. I looked at her and wanted her so bad I could taste the desire rising in my throat. My hotel room, and her hair on my pillow. A muscle worked in my jaw.

"There has to be a way, Bill."

"I can't find it."

Her eyes dropped. "So we can go to hell then. Go to hell, go directly to hell, do not pass Go, do not collect two hundred dollars."

"You mean go to jail, don't you?"

"This is the adult version. Monopoly for hippies."

The idea was there all at once. Small talk had triggered it, and then the whole scheme was there, fully developed, perfect. Would I have thought of it sooner or later anyway? A good question.

"Bill? What's the matter?"

"Go to jail," I said.

"I don't get it."

"I do," I said. "And it's pretty."

6

She dropped me at the avenue. I picked up the rental and headed for the hotel, then changed my mind and took a left turn. I drove through the Negro neighborhood and into the old Polish neighborhood, and I sat on a stool in a tavern and drank boilermakers for a few hours. The tavern was painted a bright yellow on the outside, and the interior was done in equally bright red and blue. It was enough to blind you. I drank slowly and steadily, tossed a handful of nickels into an illegal pinball machine, tossed a handful of dimes into a legal bowling machine, and had a sandwich of Polish sausage on black bread.

It was a cool and windless evening. I didn't want to think about Murray Rogers or Joyce Rogers, and if I had gone back to the hotel I would have thought of little else. The Polish tavern was a handy escape. I bought the first two drinks myself, and then I taught a pair of steelworkers how to play the old match game, and after that they did most of the buying. In the end I was drunk enough to have trouble fitting the key into the car's ignition, but still sober enough to drive it once I had the key business mastered. I reached the hotel and fell asleep when I touched the bed.

In the morning I showered and shaved and put on a clean suit and a sincere tie. I had breakfast in the coffee shop downstairs. I was a little bit hungover but the food and the coffee took away the bite. I winked at the waitress, left a good tip, and found a phone booth.

It was around ten. Main Street was heavy with traffic and the buses were rolling along and smelling up the air. A batch of teenage girls, lipsticked and jean clad, were oohing over a department store's window display. I turned into the phone booth, sat down, dropped a dime in the slot and called Murray Rogers at his office.

"Bill Maynard," I told the girl. I dangled on the line while she told Rogers who was calling, and then he was giving me a large hello.

"I'd like to see you this afternoon," I said. "If I could."

"Trouble?"

"No trouble. I still haven't made that trip to New York. I've been thinking that maybe I'd like to hang around here, find a niche for myself and get settled."

He was enthusiastic, told me he hadn't been kidding when he said he'd like to see me stay in town. "I've got a luncheon appointment," he said. "It will tie me up from one until about two-thirty. But any time after that is fine."

"I'll be up around two-thirty, then."

"Good," he said. "I'll see you, Bill."

The main library was on Panmore Square near the hotel. I felt a little out of place there. The card sharp doesn't lead a life that keeps him in the literary swim; I knew a blackjack dealer in Vegas who thought *Mechanix Illustrated* was a card sharp's manual with photographs, for example. But I made myself at home and took a run through the card catalogue, jotting down a few titles on a yellow slip of paper. I gave the slip to an auburn-haired librarian named Lenore Something-Or-Other, and she handed it to a beady-eyed page, and he brought me half of my requested books a few minutes later and explained that the other half were out somewhere. I carried the books to a table and skimmed through them. I picked up an idea here, a notion there.

Ideas and notions with a purpose. Because we had managed to hit on the right way to have our cake and eat it, too, the perfect ploy for moving Murray out of the picture without our letting go of his money. It was simple, really.

We would send him to jail.

At a quarter to two I gave the books back to stack and left. I grabbed a hamburger and coffee and didn't even try to cheat the cashier. Murray Rogers had an office in the Rand Building, which was as close as the city came to a skyscraper. The building was some twenty-eight stories tall and his office was on the twenty-fourth floor. I rode up in an express elevator and walked in through a frosted-glass door with his name on it. A pair of green leather chairs framed a table piled high with old copies of *Fortune* and *Esquire.* There was a receptionist sitting behind a heavy oak desk. She was neatly starched and crisply antiseptic. I gave her my name and she put it on the intercom. I heard Rogers' voice tell her to send me in. She pointed me at another frosted-glass door with his name on it and the word Private as subtitle. I stepped inside and he stood up and we shook hands. I passed up a cigar, accepted a drink. I sat down and we smiled earnestly at each other.

"So you like it here," he said. "I'm glad to hear that, Bill. Have you been looking for work?"

"Not exactly, Murray. I've been feeling my way around."

He nodded. "Sy said something about you—uh, sort of checking out the classifieds. What are you looking for? Plastics?"

It was time to drop the plastic front before somebody realized that I couldn't tell my acetate from a hole in the ground. "I'm not exactly sold on plastics," I said. "That was my last job, but I haven't really spent that much time in the field. And I don't see any real future in it myself. You need a strong engineering background or some grounding in chemistry to rise close to the top. Otherwise it's just a sales slot forever without much room to grow."

"And you want something with a future."

"That's right."

"Well, that goes with settling down," Murray said. "A man can drift around and take things easy for just so long. Then it all seems empty that way. It's fine when you're young and not so fine as you get older. A wife and children and a home become very important then." He chuckled. "I suppose I sound pretty fatherly, don't I? I've got a few years on you but not enough to play papa. Uncle, maybe."

Uncle was better, I thought. The other way was too damned Oedipal—sending the old man to the pen and marrying Mama. And Joyce made a lousy mother figure.

"I'd like to give you a hand," Murray Rogers said. "Maybe I like the idea of guiding someone else toward success. It would be a source of vicarious pleasure, I think. I've already made my own success. It would be nice to watch a younger man do the same thing."

It sounded sincere enough but there was an undercurrent of smugness that irritated me. I don't know. Maybe I was searching for reasons to hate the man. But he was telling me how tidily he had made his own pile and was at the same time operating under the tacit assumption that with his guidance I couldn't help doing well for myself. That kind of attitude is one of the privileges of the successful man. I still resented it.

We spent an hour and a half figuring out a job for

me. I invented mythical experience and awarded myself a mythical college degree. By the time we were finished he had managed to figure out half a dozen spots for me, all of them with room for advancement and none of them paying less than ten grand a year for a starter. Nothing less would have been considered—I was going to be a friend of his, a hand in his poker game, a member of his country club. Naturally I couldn't be expected to live on his scale, but I had to come close enough to be a suitable member in his social circle. Ten thousand dollars a year was minimal.

Besides that, the occupation had to be socially acceptable in that class. I couldn't be a salesman on a used-car lot, couldn't pump gas, couldn't fix broken bicycles. The professions were out because I didn't have the training. What was left was high-level selling or some phase of management—something like that.

And Murray did manage to hit six or seven jobs that fit. The whole thing threw me a little, to tell the truth. The country is filled with people fighting their way up the shaky ladder of success, studying nights to move from eighty-five to ninety bucks a week. And just because I happened to know a guy casually and because he knew a lot of other people, I could step into a slot that would be worth ten to fifteen grand a year, all with no previous experience and no aptitude more far-reaching than an ability to make intelligent conversation and a good poker personality.

It was all so much a violation of the Horatio Alger ethic that I paid an undue amount of attention to it. But I had time to lead the conversation where I wanted it, which was toward the colorful career of one Murray Rogers, attorney-at-law. That was the point of the whole interview. I was going to need a job if I was going to spend time on our little gambit, but more important I was going to have to know a lot about Rogers. Enough to find the hook that would send him to jail. If he had actually done something criminal, that would be ideal. The ideal, however, was a little too much to hope for. All we really needed was a good iron-clad method for framing him.

Because jail would be perfect. He could be jailed for anything, just so long as it didn't carry the death penalty. It didn't much matter how much time he spent in the tank. Once he was there, we had it made with no sweat at all. She could either milk his holdings so that his cash was in our pockets by the time he got out, or she could divorce him. It didn't matter how great a lawyer he was if he were in jail. Convicts can't bargain from a position of strength. There wasn't a court in Nevada that wouldn't give her most of his dough on any grounds she wanted to name.

I learned a lot of things about him that afternoon. I learned that he made his money on his own, that he built himself up from nothing. I learned that he had a few law grads who researched his cases. I learned that he and Ed Hart frequently worked in tandem, with Hart preparing returns and Murray fighting out the legal hassles. I learned the names of a few of his clients, and I found out what local restaurants he preferred, and I found out that he had his hair cut at the Statler barbershop. I learned all this and more, but I didn't learn anything that gave me an angle.

I also learned just how much he hated to lose. Around four he opened the top drawer of his desk and dragged out a deck of cards. He riffled through them a few times and looked up at me.

"You play gin rummy, Bill?"

"I used to. I haven't played in awhile."

"Care to play a game?"

"Sure."

"Say a quarter of a cent a point?" He grinned. "I'm hustling you, fellow. Gin's my game. But I've got to try and make up for that beating you handed me at the poker table."

He was still thinking about the poker game. That was the kind of man he was—he wasn't used to losing, not at anything. In business or cards or love, he was used to coming out on top.

We played one set, Hollywood, spades doubled, the works. Gin is a subtle game, and he hadn't been kidding when he said it was his game. It's a funny thing about gin—everybody who plays it thinks that he's fairly good at it. You'll find men who will admit that they're lousy bridge players, or mediocre poker players, or bad golfers, or whatever. You'll never hear anyone describe himself as a lousy gin player. God knows why.

Another thing, the average Joe thinks that the game is all luck, or mostly luck, and this is wrong. It's not a test of character like poker or a science like bridge, but a good player will beat a poor player eight sets out of ten.

It is also the easiest game on earth as far as a card cheat is concerned. There are half a hundred small gambits, any of them geared to give you the best of it in the course of a game. Peeks, minor-league deck stacking, a card or two palmed and held out—any of these bits makes the difference in a hand.

I was too interested in Murray Rogers himself to pay too much attention to the cards. If you play the game seriously you have to remember every card and think things out fairly far in advance, and I didn't want to bother. I played a sloppy game and rigged things just enough to come out six bucks to the good. The son of a gun couldn't help scowling while he added up the score.

"You play a good game," he said.

"I was lucky. I held good cards."

"Sometimes that's all it takes." He paid me a five and a one. "We'll have to do this again," he said.

Afterward I called the local office of Dun & Bradstreet and asked for a full credit report on Murray

Rogers. They knew him and said they could have a brief ready the next afternoon. I gave a false name and told them I'd stop by for it.

That was Monday. On Tuesday I didn't do much of anything besides consuming the standard amount of food and catching a double feature at the movie near the library. Late in the afternoon I went over to D & B to pick up their report. The fee was fifteen bucks, which seemed reasonable enough. But after I paid I riffled through the bills in my wallet. Money was running out again, slowly but steadily. I thought about this on the way back to the Panmore, and then I leaned against the side of a handy building and started to laugh.

It was funny. I needed that job Murray was going to dig up for me. There was a poker game in a few days but I couldn't afford to cheat in it. If anything, I had to manage to lose a minimum of twenty dollars. When you're playing for a few hundred grand, you can't afford to cheat in a dollar-limit game. So I needed a job: I had to have it in order to job Murray properly.

In my room I read through the three pages from the Dun & Bradstreet people. Murray wasn't a bad credit risk, not at all. He owned the house free and clear and he had bought it a few years ago for forty-five thou. He kept about fifty grand in the stock market, mostly in fairly steady stuff with a few electronics issues mixed in for capital gains potential. He owned a lot of real property in the city—a trio of cheap residential hotels on Chippewa, a third of a forty-eight-lane suburban bowling alley, a piece of a new office building on Delaware Avenue. There was money tied up in high-yield syndications, money in a whole host of savings banks, money in his personal checking account and money in his business account. There was, all in all, a lot of money.

I committed sections of the report to memory, then tucked it away where nobody would be likely to trip over it. I went out and had dinner at one of Murray Rogers' favorite restaurants. Then I wandered downtown and paid a buck and a half to the box-office girl at the Palace Burlesque and went inside to watch the strippers thrust their groins at me.

The strippers were a bore. I had known one once, a second-rater who played some of the Fifty-Second Street tourist traps in New York. She had lived in a three-room walkup on West Seventy-Third near the park, and she had had a ten-year-old boy who wasn't too clear on what she did for a living. For a period of about a month I shared her bed afternoons while the kid was in school. It had been exciting at first; she was a stripper and strippers are supposed to be exciting—that's part of the American Dream. But she had been mindless and soulless and dead inside, and in spite of the thousand sexual tricks a thousand men had taught her, she had been every bit as frigid as death. So the strippers were a bore. If they did anything, they reminded me I wanted Joyce. That I needed her.

But there was a magician on the bill. He was around fifty. I didn't recognize him but his name rang some sort of distant bell; I'd probably heard it when I was in the business myself. His tailcoat was frayed and his face was a map of blue alcohol lines and I looked at him and saw what I might have been if a dark-eyed man in Miami hadn't had a proposition for me.

A grim prospect. But my watching him made my fingers itch for a tall silk hat and a rabbit to yank out of it. And he wasn't even very good. He had a lot of stage presence but his moves were fairly obvious and his bag of tricks was a skimpy one. There was only one bit he had that I wasn't able to figure, a routine involving a batch of Christmas-tree ornaments that disappeared into each other, something like that. And I could tell he wasn't really essential to the trick. It was just a cute piece of equipment I didn't happen to be familiar with.

A man nudged me. I turned and looked at him. He would have been a good ad for Alcoholics Anonymous; he was drunk, and he looked unhappy about it. "Say," he said, "now how do you figure he done that?"

"What?"

"The trick," he said. "What he did with them balls,

making 'em do that and all. Now how could a man go and do something like that?"

"It's magic," I said.

"Yeah, but how's he do it?'

"It's the wand," I said.

"It's something special, the wand?"

"Sure," I said. "It's magic."

7

On Wednesday morning the phone woke me. The voice was Murray's.

"Hi, kid," he said. "Listen, I've got something good for you. You have a free day today?"

"Sure."

"Can you get over here around a quarter to twelve? I'm setting up a lunch appointment with Perry Carver for you. Perry's running an outfit called Black Sand Syndications. They sell limited partnerships in real estate syndications. It's been a big thing in New York City but it's a fairly new form of investment around here. You can get around ten percent on an investment and most of it is tax-free. I was speaking to him yesterday. He needs a good salesman or two and there's no previous experience necessary because the field is a fairly new one here. He'll take you out to lunch and you can see how it looks to you."

"It sounds good," I said.

"It might not be bad at all. Wear a suit and brush your hair and smile like a good boy. You might wind up with a pretty good position."

I wore a suit and brushed my hair and practiced smiling at myself in the mirror. I skipped breakfast and spent the rest of the morning in the library scanning everything I could find on the scintillating subject of real-estate syndication. I dodged through a book or two on the subject and checked out what some back issues of the financial magazines had to say about it. After a quick cup of coffee on Main Street I presented myself to Murray Rogers for inspection.

"You look lovely," he said in his office. "Come on, I'll take you downstairs and introduce you to Perry. Then I'll move out of your way and you two can see what develops."

Black Sand Syndications had a large office on the seventeenth floor of the same building. We took an elevator downstairs and Murray introduced me to Carver. He was a hefty man, bald on top, with innocent blue eyes and a firm jaw. His handshake was strictly dead-fish but his eyes took me in quickly. Murray made some jokes that weren't particularly funny, and I showed my capped teeth in a smile, and Carver wound up taking me to the Downtown Merchant's Club for lunch.

We had martinis first. Then I ordered a ham steak and he ordered an open turkey sandwich. He told the ancient waiter to bring us another pair of martinis. The drinks came, then the food. We ate and drank and made small talk. We were working on coffee before he said the first word about business.

"Know anything about syndicates, Maynard?"

"A little."

"Suppose you tell me what you know. That way I won't feed you a lot of information you've already got under your belt."

I played parrot for ten minutes. I regurgitated the library's store of information and told him just what a syndication was and just why it was a good investment for certain people. I told him the potentials above and beyond the tax-sheltered return, mentioned a few syndicates that had converted into common-stock corporations, and generally ran off at the mouth. The blue eyes became progressively more interested as I steamed along. By the time I was finished, Carver was beaming.

"Well, I'll be damned," he said. "You actually know the field, don't you?"

"Not really."

"Where did you learn all that? Murray mentioned you were in Chicago before you came here, said something about a plastics firm. You in investments before that?"

It seemed like a silly time to lie. Perry Carver was a man who had pushed into a new field and was doing nicely in it. I guessed he'd be more impressed by quick learning ability than experience. I told him I hadn't known a thing about syndicating a few hours ago, but picked it all up by reading a few books. For a few seconds he just stared at me. Then he started to laugh.

"I'm a son of a bitch," he said. "You know what I have to go through to find a salesman who knows his rear end from third base? I'll tell you, Maynard, I look at about twenty applications a week. None of them know the first thing. They just want to make money, that's all. And the damned fools don't know anything and can't learn anything. I tried to set up a training program to drum a few facts into their heads. Didn't work at all. I've got three decent salesmen working out of an office that could support ten of them but I can't find seven more worth putting behind a desk. You already put together more than any of those lardheads got out of the program. Can you sell?"

"I think so."

"Suppose you had a young fellow who told you he was more interested in growth than income. What would you tell him?"

He gave me a cigarette and a light. I took a drag, blew out smoke. "I'd tell him ten percent was more growth than he could expect to make in the market, and with a lot less risk. And I'd tell him that Glickman went from seven-and-a-half to thirteen or fourteen over-the-counter after conversion to a stock issue, and I'd name a few other syndicates that showed comparable performance."

"Right," he said. "Suppose your prospect was a widow with twenty thousand dollars in a savings bank. She's afraid of risk. What do you tell her?"

"That the risk is low because she'll be owning a piece of real property, not just a bag of dreams. And that the difference between four percent and ten percent is the difference between eight hundred dollars and two thousand dollars annually."

"You've got a job," Perry Carver said.

I had a job. He took me back to the Rand Building and gave me a desk next to the water cooler. He wrote out a check to me for five hundred dollars as an advance against commissions to be earned in the future. He handed me twenty cards from the prospect file, gave me a stack of letterheads and told me where to have business cards printed up.

"Make as many calls as you can," he said. "You rarely sell anybody on the first trip—that's one of the reasons I wanted to feed you an advance. I won't expect results right off the bat. If you run out of dough, just holler. And feel free to hit any side prospects you want. Don't be reluctant to sell your friends. The package we're handling now is an attractive one. New York office building, Madison Avenue and Forty-Fifth Street. It's a hundred percent rented and the distributions are personally guaranteed by the general partners for the first five years. It yields eleven percent. See what you can do, Bill."

I stayed at my desk all afternoon. I called prospects, mailed prospectuses at them, told them to look them over and that I would call in a day or two for an appointment. I made notations in an appointment calendar, jotted down trivia on each of the prospect cards. I mailed propaganda to the men in the poker game—Sy Daniels, Harold Barnes, all of them. Maybe I got carried away.

That night I dodged a dinner invitation and took myself to a steak house. It was a small club with wood paneling on the walls and big leather chairs around polished oak tables. There was a crowd at the bar. I took a table in back and polished off a thick sirloin with a baked potato. I drank scotch first and brandy afterward and smoked a few cigarettes.

After dinner I sat there and thought about Murray Rogers. I'd been dodging the issue all afternoon. It was easy to become wrapped up in the new job and forget all about the real purpose, especially easy because I liked myself better as William Maynard, bright young salesman with Black Sand Syndications. I liked that man better than Bill "Wizard" Maynard, a slick sharper who was sleeping with another man's wife and planning to send that man to jail.

I went back to the Panmore and picked up some sleep. In the morning I made a few calls and set up two afternoon appointments. I had a bite sent up from the coffee shop down the street and ate at my desk. Then I stopped to see Murray.

"I wanted to get in touch with you earlier," I said, "but I've been busy as hell."

"I spoke to Carver. Congratulations, Bill."

"Thanks."

"You really swept Perry off his feet. He was impressed, and he doesn't impress that easily. Think you'll like the work?"

"I think so."

He drummed the desk top with his fingers. "Time for a hand or three?"

"Just barely."

He took out the cards and we played a few hands of gin. I let him win a few dollars and I paid him. He boxed the cards and put them away. I took my cigarettes from my jacket pocket. There was a key on the top of his desk about midway between us. The key to his office, I guessed. I shook the cigarette pack clumsily and three or four of the cigarettes jarred loose and bounced across his desk. The two of us reached for them and scooped them up, and by the time they were back in the pack his key was in my pocket. The hand is quicker than the eye, gentlemen. A little misdirection is a dangerous thing.

There was a little booth in a parking lot on Washington Street where they made duplicate keys while-u-waited. I had the locksmith knock out a copy of Murray's key and put it on my key ring. Then I was ready for my appointments.

It was the right kind of afternoon. I kept my two appointments and both prospects were perfect ones.

The first was a fellow about my age, a cautious type who functioned as a bookkeeper. His mother had died a month or two ago and he had come into twenty-five thousand dollars worth of insurance money. He was earning seventy-five bucks a week, he wanted a second income to make life a little fuller, and he was scared to death of the stock market. My pitch on the eleven percent return appealed to him. He might have been good for the whole twenty-five grand, but I told him not to throw all of his eggs in one omelet. I sold him a pair of five-thousand dollar units and told him I'd keep my eyes open for the next good package that came our way.

The second prospect didn't have that kind of money to play with. He was a little older, and his capital was savings, not insurance windfall. He liked the idea of tax-free income and took a half-unit at twenty-five hundred dollars. He wrote me his check and I returned to the office to report to Carver.

"I can't believe it," he said. "You're terrific."

"I didn't have that much to do with it," I said. "They were pretty much pre-sold."

"Knock off for the rest of the day, Bill. Drop your hotel and find an apartment. And don't try to dodge taking credit where it's due. Don't give me that pre-sold crap. You made the calls and you closed the sales. You're a wizard, Bill."

Wizard, I thought. Sure, I thought. That's what I am—a wizard. Also a magician.

I thought I'd tell Murray about the sales and did. I accepted the congratulations and told him I'd see him at the game later that evening. When I left his office the key was right back on his desk where it belonged. He had never missed it. I had a copy and he had the original back and he didn't know a thing about it.

The game was at Ken Jameson's house. Ken was the one who headed an insurance agency. He was a few years younger than most of the other players, just about my age. He had a wife and three young kids and a house in the suburbs. We sat around the dining-room table and played poker. Ken's wife was a pretty girl who had sprung full-blown from the forehead of some slick magazine editor. She took care of the kids, put them to bed, and parked herself upstairs in front of the television set for the evening. She didn't venture into the dining room except to say hello. She wouldn't have recognized a bottom deal in slow motion.

If we had played at Ken's house that first night, I would have been in New York a day later. There would have been no electric contact with Joyce Rogers, no job with Carver's outfit, no dark mystery of frames and set-ups. Life is a hellishly iffy proposition from beginning to end. There are always a million sneaky little variables, and any one of them can send you spinning in another direction entirely.

We played, and I didn't cheat. My restraint was not

easy to maintain at first. But I managed, and at nine-thirty I was about fifteen dollars in the hole.

I pushed back my chair, straightened up. "You'll have to excuse me for about an hour," I explained. "I've got a call I have to make, a plant foreman over on the East Side. This was the only time I could arrange to see him."

"That's a hell of a note," Murray said. "We were just starting to take a few dollars away from you."

"I'll be back before eleven. I'll lose in a hurry to make up for it."

"A real go-getter," Sy Daniels said. "Don't you know the rules? No business on Friday nights. Just poker."

I laughed, left and boarded the Corvair. I started the car and pulled away and headed back into town.

There was no foreman over on the East Side. Correction—there were probably a few hundred foremen over on the East Side, but none of them interested me at the moment. I had other plans.

I drove the car, smoked a cigarette. That was a nice thing about my new job—it gave me a free and easy sort of schedule. I could knock off work whenever I pleased if I had something else going, and at the same time I could invent a business appointment whenever I needed an excuse. I needed one now.

The car seemed to know the way. I finished my cigarette and pitched out the butt. In the morning I would have to see about finding an apartment—the

Panmore could run into money if I stayed there any length of time. And pretty soon it would be time to turn the rental back to Hertz and make a down payment on a car of my own.

I made a final turn, drove part of the way down the block. I eased the car over to the curb, braked, killed the ignition. I walked fifty yards or so to stand in front of a big brick ranch on a large plot. There were a few lights on. The garage door was open and I could see a Caddy convertible parked there. She was home.

The night was cool, clear. At the front door I poked the bell. *My Dog Has Fleas,* the chimes played.

Joyce Rogers opened the door. Her eyes widened and her mouth opened and she started to say something, but I pushed her inside and drew the door shut and stopped whatever she was going to say with a kiss.

I held her close, felt the sweet warmth of her fine body against mine. I unpinned her chestnut hair and it fell free. I ran my fingers through it.

"We've got about an hour," I said. "Let's not waste it."

8

"You're crazy, Wizard. Insane!"

"Why?"

"Right here. In his own house. It's not safe, Wizard."

"He's at the game," I said. "He won't be leaving. And the girls will be out for awhile yet."

"How do you know?"

"He mentioned it during the game. Don't worry about it, Joyce. Don't worry about a thing."

"But—"

"Or don't you want me?"

"Oh, God!"

I reached for her, caught her by her shoulders. She held back for a moment, then fell against me, all warm and trembling. I ran my hands over her body and her flesh quivered.

"The bedroom—" Joyce started to say.

We never made the bedroom. There was a couch on the other side of the living room, but we didn't reach there, either. I kissed her and she tossed her arms around my neck and clung to me like ivy to a stone wall. The stone wall melted and we sank to the floor and held each other close.

I put my hand under her skirt and touched the silky perfection of her thighs. Her legs opened and I stroked her high on the inside of one thigh until she was moaning hysterically. She pushed me aside and yanked her skirt up around her waist. I took her panties off. She fell back on the floor, her eyes rolling, her forehead dotted with perspiration.

"Now," she moaned. "Now, now, right now, Bill, now, now—"

No kisses, no sweet caresses, no little bits and pieces. I fell on her like a tree.

There was all that aching, all that need, and it exploded for us like a truckload of nitro on a cobblestone road. There was nothing soft or gentle, nothing remotely sweet about our love-making. What we had was something you couldn't deny or postpone, something you could never push out of the way or ignore. And it was not the sort of blissful idyll that would evolve easily and naturally into a pattern of three or four pleasant bangs per week in the master bedroom of a split-level shack. Fires that burn with the Bill Maynard-Joyce Rogers type of flame don't simmer down.

Which could have been a hint, a clue, a flashed card. But maybe I wasn't looking.

Afterward she pulled on her panties and pulled down her skirt and we sat on the couch and talked. She had most of my story already from Murray. I gave her the rest and slipped her a quick summary of the plan of action. She liked it. Her approval showed in her eyes, bright and excited.

I lit a cigarette. "Of course," I said, "we could forget it."

She said nothing, and that noncommittally.

"I'm all set up in business," I told her. "I even enjoy my work. I could just stick to my job and make enough money to keep me happy. And you could go on being Murray Rogers' loving wife. We've both got it fairly soft, you know. We're not in an especially desperate situation."

"And keep seeing each other like this?"

"Why not?"

"And never try for the brass ring? And stay tied up like this? You like your work because it's temporary, Wizard. It's part of the act, not something you'd have to be doing for the rest of your life. You might not like it so much that way."

I avoided her eyes. The whole routine had started out as a joke, but somehow or other I had been saying things I partly meant. After all, I did like the work. And the idea of jobbing Murray Rogers was becoming less attractive the better I knew him.

"It was just a gag," I said.

"Was it?"

"Sure."

"It's a bad kind of joke, Wizard." She took one of my hands in both of hers. "This is too big for me to joke about it, Wizard. I'm in this all the way. We've both got to be in it all the way."

On the way back to the game I tried to concentrate on driving the Corvair. That wasn't easy. I kept telling myself that my semi-pitch to Joyce about playing our future straight had just been a gag. I was no real-estate syndicator. I was a sharp, a quick-money boy, a guy whose world spun faster than the rest of the planet Earth. I wanted the fast money and the fast action and the fast women. Hotel rooms, ashes on the floor.

Back at the game I complained about a stupid foreman who couldn't understand anything no matter how long you hammered it into his skull. I played poker until the game broke up around two-thirty and I wound up forty-five dollars in the hole. Then I drove back to the hotel and slept.

I looked at three apartments before I found the one I wanted. It was on College Street—two rooms and a bath and kitchenette, all furnished in Early American ugliness. The wallpaper was floral and the rugs were imitation Orientals. What the hell, I was renting the place, not buying it. The apartment might not be designed to turn on an interior decorator but it was roomy and comfortable and convenient and that was all I wanted. I paid a month's rent, talked my way out of signing a lease. I moved my stuff over from the hotel and I was in business.

By midafternoon I had given back the Corvair to

the Hertz people and had put a hundred dollars down on a two-year-old Ford. It wasn't exactly a dream car either but it was way ahead of the Corvair and the payments were only a tiny gouge per month. At three o'clock I drove downtown and parked in a lot a block from the Rand Building. I rode the elevator to the seventeenth floor.

Black Sand's office was closed Saturdays but Carver had given me a key and had told me to use the office any time I felt like it. I unlocked the door. Nobody was around. I rearranged some junk on my desk just to show I had been there, then left to climb seven flights of stairs. It would have been easier to use the elevator, but elevator operators occasionally remember people and I didn't want to be remembered. I was tired by the time I hit the twenty-fourth floor. I leaned against a wall and let my breathing go back to normal.

The lights were off in Murray's office. The door was locked. I waited until the hallway was empty and silent, then used the duplicate key. The door opened. Once inside, I closed the door. The same key opened Murray's private office, next on the agenda. I didn't turn the light on. There was enough light to see by, and it was no time to attract any attention at all.

I sat behind his desk. There was a typewriter in a well to the left of me. I swung it out, took onionskin and letterhead and carbon paper from the center drawer, made a sandwich out of them and put it in the typewriter. A cigarette would have been nice. I didn't light one.

I put Monday's date on the top of the page. Then I typed—

Jack:

What do you know about a man named August Milani? He called me in reference to the Whitlock matter and demanded payment. Have you any idea who he is? Please let me know immediately as to the best course of action.

Murray Rogers

I rolled the sandwich out of the typewriter and slipped the carbon paper between a fresh sheet of letterhead and a fresh piece of onionskin. I read the letter through again and nodded. It had the right tone.

The second letter was dated four days later. It read—

Jack:

Milani seems to have us over a barrel. He says he's fully prepared to go to the IRS boys, since the department will pay a percentage of recovered funds to informers in cases of this nature. I've decided to agree to his terms in the hope that this is the last we'll hear from him.

Murray

The third letter was dated the following Monday.

It was the hardest to write, and I gave it three tries before I got the phrasing just the way I wanted it. It wound up like this—

Jack:

Don't worry about A.M. The man's not willing to settle for what I've given him thus far, and seems to possess an insatiable appetite. By the time you receive this letter he'll have been accommodated in the only manner possible.

M.R.

I put away the typewriter and straightened up the desk. I took the carbons and the letterheads and the onionskins with me and slipped out of the office, locking it behind me. I walked down seven fights of stairs—it was easier going down than up. The elevator came. I rode to the lobby and walked out to my car. I ran the Ford to my new apartment, stuck the car in a parking place. The apartment felt like home already. I had a cigarette then and smoked it all the way down.

I re-examined the letters. They were on his stationery and were worded just as he would write them. The letters had been typed on his typewriter. They didn't have his signature, but nobody signs carbons. And I was interested in the copies, not the originals.

I shredded the sheets of letterhead and flushed them down the toilet. I did the same with the carbons. Then I put the onionskin copies away in a bureau drawer. They would be useful, but for the time being I didn't need them. They were props. When the rest of the stage was set I could put the props to use.

I drove across Main Street just before the shops closed for the day. I turned off, parked in a store lot and visited a few shops and bought a few things. The neighborhood was one of those marginal areas you find near the downtown business section of any good-sized city. Main Street was a few blocks to the west. Skid Row was around the corner. The Negro neighborhood ran north and east. In the middle was a snatch of surplus stores and hockshops and numbers drops and cheap bars. I didn't figure to run into any business friends around there.

I bought a third-hand valise and a second-hand Broadway suit. I stuffed the valise with the suit and added a few shirts and a pair of beat-up shoes. I bought a new hat, black with a very short brim, which I crammed into the valise. The more beat-up the hat looked, the better. I added a flashy half-dollar tie, a showy and cheap signet ring. I stuffed everything into the valise and tossed it into the Ford and drove home.

From a drugstore phone booth I called the telephone company and asked them to install a phone in my apartment on Monday. Then I dropped another dime in the slot and called the Panmore to find out if there were any messages for me. There was one—I was supposed to call Seymour Daniels as soon as possible. I did. Mary Daniels answered and said hello very happily when she found out who was calling.

"Just a minute," she said. "I'll let you talk to Sy."

I waited, started a cigarette. Then Sy was on, cheerful and noisy.

"Good to talk to you," he said. "Got stung a little last night, didn't you?"

"I gave a little money back."

Sy laughed. "Pretty good game," he said. "Say, I was wondering. Do you play bridge or is poker your only game?"

"I've played bridge," I said. "Why?"

"Well, this girl Mary's friendly with is dropping over tonight, see, and I thought you might like to make a fourth. It won't be a very exciting evening, just cards and drinks and conversation. But the girl's nice. You might enjoy yourself."

It was the old conspiracy of the married against the single. There was a friend of Mary's and there was me, and why not get the two of us together? I don't need your friend, I thought. I'm busy making it with Murray's wife.

"Sounds fine," I said.

"We'll expect you around nine?"

"Right. I don't know how good my game will be, though. I haven't played in a hell of a while."

"Don't worry about it," he said heartily. "It doesn't make much difference how you play."

I managed to slip off the line before he could realize how funny his last statement was. It was true—it didn't make a hell of a difference whether I played like Charlie Goren or the North Park Every-Other-Tuesday Ladies' Bridge League. Bridge wasn't the important part of the evening. I was being fixed up with somebody, and that was more important than a deck of cards.

My bridge game turned out to be lousy. This didn't surprise me. I had never played the game honestly in my life. Bridge happens to be the easiest game in the world for a cheater if only because communication between partners is a significant element in the play. You can cheat with a million various signals, and you don't have to rely on card manipulation or anything of the sort. I would have played the game more often if there hadn't been such difficulties in arranging a stakes game. Anyone who plays money bridge with strangers deserves whatever happens to him. You can be cheated forever and never know it.

All of which is intended to explain the fact I played a lousy game at Sy's house. We played in the living room with soft music in the background, and Sy and Mary partners against Barb and me. That was my partner—Barbara Lambert, thirty-two, high school

English teacher, married once and divorced now, no children.

She was a pretty blonde with a settled look to her. At the outset of the evening she seemed every bit as uncomfortable as she had every right to be, given her situation. She was an unmarried gal who was being fixed up by a friend, and this is not exactly a position of strength. But she warmed up and relaxed as the evening went on. Maybe my lousy playing encouraged her.

We played three rubbers of bridge, and in each one Sy and Mary beat us silly. They seemed a little embarrassed by the time they polished us off for the third straight time, so we put the cards away and sat around playing conversation. That wasn't difficult. Barb was a sweet kid, intelligent if not especially hip, and we managed to keep the verbal ball going. Sy and I locked into a long discussion about the relative merits of mutual funds and syndications, and at the end of all this Mary poured coffee. We drank up and called it an evening. Mary had driven over to pick up Barb, a clever move designed to leave me with the chore of trucking her home again. I didn't mind.

I drove slowly. She was quiet, sitting with her head back and the wind playing with her hair. I switched on the radio and we listened to rock and roll for a horrible moment. Then I switched off the radio.

She said, "Bill?"

I waited.

"I had a nice time," she said.

"So did I."

"It was a strange evening."

"How?"

"Staged. All set up and arranged. At first I had the feeling that we were all reading dialogue that somebody else had written out for us ages ago."

She stopped talking. I turned at the corner and she told me when we were at her house. I stopped the Ford and took her to the door and she didn't say anything until we were standing on the steps.

Then she said, "Married couples do that all the time. They think they have to take people like us and bring us together so that we can get married and make babies and live fuller lives. Even if—if it worked, well, it would make a person feel as though someone else were arranging his life for him."

I didn't say anything. Her eyes were directed at me but she was staring past me, off into space. Her lips parted slightly. She looked as though she wanted to be kissed and it seemed like a good idea, so I kissed her. She was stiff at first. Then she relaxed slightly and then I let go of her. Her cheeks were slightly flushed.

Barb said, "That was—nice, Bill."

"I'll call you soon."

"You don't have to, you know."

"I know. I'll want to."

"I think I'd like that," she said.

I turned away and drove home. I would call Barb, of course. The action would be a good cover. If I were dating a girl, people would be less likely to imagine anything between Joyce and myself. So I would call Barb Lambert, and I would go out with her.

In another world I would have married her, and we would have sold beautiful syndications together, and she'd be the beneficiary of my life insurance policy. She was living in that world. I wasn't.

I slept late on Sunday. It was past noon when I awoke and I was hungry. I made it around the corner and bought breakfast food at a deli, lox and bagel and instant coffee. I ate, showered, and fancied a different set of clothes.

The second-hand Broadway suit was a little tight on me. That was fine. I took off the jacket, dropped it and walked on it. I picked up the jacket, then, and brushed it off and slipped it on again. I tossed the hat down and stepped on it, grinding some dirt into the felt. I straightened the hat out again, wiped it fairly clean. When I was finished, the chapeau looked as though I had owned it for ages.

I knotted on the loud tie and toned it down with coffee stains. I stuffed my feet into the broken-down shoes and tied them. I checked myself in the mirror, tugged the hat down over my eyes. I looked shabby and seedy and not at all like me.

In a drugstore I bought a pair of glasses with plain lenses. They added a final touch. I carried my valise a few blocks south and a few blocks east. There were six hotels in a row on the cheap street and all looked appropriate for the second-hand suit and the battered hat. I tried three hotels before I found just what I wanted.

The third one was the charm. It was called the Glade, and the rooms rented for two bucks a night or ten bucks a week. I walked through what passed for a lobby with my head tossed back and my shoulders hunched forward. I leaned a shoulder against the desk and looked at the desk clerk. When I talked to him my voice sounded like all the wrong parts of Brooklyn, and my lips didn't move much.

"I need a room," I said. "Only I got no use for stairs. You got anything on the first floor?"

The other hotels hadn't. The Glade did. The clerk showed me to a room in the back. There was a cigarette-scarred dresser, an army cot, a washbowl, a cracked hunk of linoleum on the floor.

"Yeah," I said. "Okay."

Out front the clerk said the room would run me two dollars a day or ten a week, payable in advance. I reached into a pants pocket and came up with two worn dollar bills. He wanted a dollar deposit for the key.

"You think I'm gonna run off with your key?" I said. "Hell—"

I gave him the deposit, but not before I had haggled with him for a few minutes to preserve appearances. He passed me a registration card and gave me a ballpoint pen. I leaned on the counter, studied the card, tapped the pen on the counter, glanced up at him.

"A few days," I said, "I won't have to stay in dumps like this one. A few days and I pull out of this town in a Cadillac. You believe that, Charlie?"

He started to tell me his name wasn't Charlie, then decided not to bother.

"You better believe it," I said. "You just better believe it. Little Augie is going to do fine."

Then I took the pen and filled out the card. *August Milani,* I wrote. *New York City.*

9

I stayed at the Glade for an hour or so, then returned to my place on College Street and belted away some sleep. In the morning I drove downtown and to work. Two salesmen were at their desks and poring over a brochure, and another salesman was jawing with someone on the phone. Perry Carver was in his private office. I made a few calls, filed three or four prospects under Call-Again-Some-Time, managed to make two appointments for the evening. Then Perry Carver called me on the intercom and I stepped into his office.

"Well," he said. "How's it going, Bill?"

"Fine."

"So fine you have to work weekends?" Carver grinned. "I'm a detective, saw your desk rearranged. That's always a good sign. This is no business for a clockwatcher, Bill. A man has to be willing to work long hours when the work is there for him and take it easy when the going is slow. I like the way you operate, Bill."

We said a few more nice things to each other. I took off about eleven, grabbed a cup of coffee at a drug-store soda fountain. There was a men's mag on the rack with a cover streamer touting an article on how to beat the crap tables at Vegas. I picked up the magazine and scanned the article. It was one of those bonehead jobs pushing the old double-up system—you double your bet every time you lose, and eventually you come out a winner. There was only one little flaw. Sooner or later you were bucking the house limit and the casino had you by the throat. I put back the magazine and crossed over to the phone booth.

Murray's girl answered the phone. I put Brooklyn back into my voice and told her to let me speak to Rogers. She asked who was calling.

"August Milani," I said.

There was a pause while she checked with Rogers. Then she said, "Sorry to keep you waiting, Mr. Milani. Could you tell me what your call is in reference to?"

"Sure, honey," I said. I chuckled lewdly. "Tell Rogers I want to talk to him about Whitlock."

Maybe Murray's curiosity was aroused. At any rate, he was on the line a few seconds later, asking what he could do for me. I waited until I heard the receptionist click herself off the line. Then I dropped the Brooklyn accent.

"My name's Milani," I said. "August Milani. Sam Whitlock suggested you might be in the market for some life insurance, Mr. Rogers. I'd like to make an appointment with you—"

"I've got all the coverage I need," he said.

"Now, that's always a moot point. If we could get together for an hour or so, Mr. Rogers—"

"I'm sorry," he said. "I'm not interested."

I was still talking earnestly when he broke the connection. I put the receiver on the hook and stayed in the booth long enough to build a fire in a cigarette. I thought of Murray telling the court that Milani was just an insurance man, a pest trying to sell him a policy, while Murray's receptionist contradicted him and said that Milani sounded like some kind of gangster.

It was getting cute.

I sat on the Carver office telephone most of the afternoon. One man thought he might buy a half-unit but he wanted to discuss the matter with his wife first. Another was interested but hadn't been able to read the brochure thoroughly yet. Would I call him in a day or two? I made a notation to do so. By four-thirty I had called everybody I felt like calling. I leaned back in my chair and smoked a cigarette. It would have been nice to call Joyce, let her know what was happening, make some plans and talk out some dreams. Nice, but also foolish. We wouldn't be seeing much of each other for the next two weeks. That was the way it had to be. If we were connected, the whole mess would cave in on us.

So I flipped through the phonebook and dialed a

number. The phone rang four times before she reached it, and her hello was on the breathless side.

"Hello yourself," I said. "This is Bill Maynard."

"Oh," Barbara Lambert said. She sounded surprised.

"I didn't know if you'd be home from school yet or not. I thought I'd give you a try."

"I was just walking through the door when the phone rang."

I didn't say anything for a minute and the silence was slightly loud. I pictured her in her small house, a comfortable blonde who lived alone, holding the telephone to her ear and waiting a little nervously to find out what I wanted. It didn't seem altogether fair to make her part of the wrapping paper on a frameup.

"I was wondering," I said.

"Yes?"

"Are you busy tomorrow night, Barb? I thought we could have dinner and take in a movie."

She said that would be very nice. She sounded pleased and maybe just a little bit giddy. I told her I would pick her up around seven. Then I cleared off my desk, said goodbye all around and left the office. I drove home. The telephone people had installed a phone for me and I called a few people to let them know my new number. Then I took a breath and called the Glade Hotel.

"Milani," I said. "August Milani. Is he in?"

My voice didn't sound quite like Rogers' voice. But it was as close as I could come. I waited while the desk clerk checked. Milani wasn't in. This didn't exactly surprise me.

"I'd like to leave a message," I said.

"Sure."

"My name is Rogers," I said. "Tell Mr. Milani his terms are impossible and I'm afraid we cannot do business."

I made him read the message back to me. Then I thanked him and broke the connection.

I took care of my evening appointments by ten. I drove the Ford back to the apartment, switched to the shabby suit and the loud tie. On the way to the Glade I pulled the hat down over my forehead and added the glasses. The desk clerk gave me the message from Rogers. I chuckled nastily and said something to the effect that the bastard wouldn't get off so easy, that he was going to pay off sooner or later. The desk clerk tried to keep a poker face but I could tell that the words had registered. He wouldn't forget them.

Tuesday and Wednesday, I kept feeding dimes into telephones. I called Murray Rogers' office four or five times, each time giving my name as Milani and asking in a hoodish tone to talk to Rogers. I got through to him once and fed him the life insurance pitch all over again and he hung up on me almost at once. The other times I didn't get past the receptionist. The poor girl must have had an interesting picture of me by then. I got nastier and nastier, and if she asked Murray about me he could only say that I was some nutty insurance salesman, a little stupider and a little more persistent than most. The girl wouldn't believe it. She was a perfect receptionist, starched and prim and proper. But she couldn't swallow a pitch like that.

I called my hotel a few times, leaving messages from Rogers, and I picked up the messages at the hotel and cackled triumphantly. The stage was setting itself up neatly.

Tuesday night I took Barb Lambert to dinner at an Italian restaurant. She had veal mozzarella and I had lobster fra diavolo and we knocked off a bottle of chianti together. The restaurant was the sort of place where David Niven and Jean Simmons always had dinner as a prelude to an illicit affair in a Hollywood bedroom farce. Candles burned in straw-covered wine bottles. Violin music melted forth from a public address system. The lights were dim.

Reality slipped away. Barbara became a little prettier, a little cleverer, less the unsure schoolteacher and more the vibrant woman. My hand crossed the table and covered hers. Her fingers were cool, soft. Her eyes shone.

"I've missed this," she said.

"This?"

"Romance. I like it, Bill."

"So do I."

"We should have met more romantically," she said lazily. "We could have been seat-partners in a transatlantic jet. You could have rescued me from a rapist in the park. Something like that. But instead we were fixed up by a pair of meddling matchmakers. That's not very romantic, is it?"

"We could always pretend."

She picked up her wine glass with her free hand and finished her chianti. "Let's," she said. "Let's pretend. Let's be different people. Instead of a schoolteacher I'll be something exciting. I'll be a call girl, all right?"

"I'll be a customer, then."

She laughed wickedly. "No, no, no," she said. "That's not romantic. I'll be a high-priced call girl. And what will you be?"

"A wealthy prince?"

"I don't think so. How about a master criminal?"

"A jewel thief?"

"Mmmmm," she said. "Perfect. And do you know how we got together? You just finished robbing a horrid old woman of a fortune in emeralds, and I just finished breaking off with my wealthy old lover, and now we're having dinner together in an intimate little spot on the Italian Riviera. Isn't that romantic?"

A movie wouldn't have been romantic enough. Instead we drove around searching for something exciting. We wound up in a jazz club. We were the only non-beats in the place and we drew stares that would have made Barb uncomfortable if it hadn't been for the wine. As it was, she didn't mind at all. We sat at a small table in front and drank dubious scotch and listened to a hard-bop quartet play funky blues.

"Romantic," she said.

A fat girl tried to sing like Dinah Washington. A uniformed cop strolled into the club, stood for a few moments surveying the place, then turned and left. Our waitress brought fresh drinks. The musicians took a break, then came back on again.

"It's getting late," Barb said.

"Close to twelve."

"And I have school tomorrow. Isn't that silly? A call girl with school tomorrow. And my handsome jewel thief has to go to the office and sell pieces of buildings, or something. I guess we're just turning into pumpkins, aren't we?"

I paid the check and left too big a tip. We ducked out of the smoky club and gulped fresh air on the street outside. In the car I started to turn the key in the ignition but she put her hand on mine and stopped me. I turned. Barb's eyes were closed, her mouth pouty. I picked up my cue and kissed her and her body shivered in my arms. Her mouth tasted of liquor and tobacco and sweet hunger. I kissed her again and she stirred in response, shifting her weight and locking her arms around my neck. My hand moved to the side of her breast. My fingers pressed the firm softness of her and she gasped with excitement.

I felt like ten different kinds of a bastard.

We didn't talk on the way back to her place. Barb sat very close to me, her head on my shoulder, her eyes shut. She was breathing heavily. I forced my mind on my driving and tried not to think about other things. It was like struggling not to think of a white rhinoceros. The thoughts were there and I couldn't shove them aside.

I stuck the Ford in her driveway and walked her to her door. I stood at her side while she opened the door. She turned to me, slowly, and I kissed her. Partly because I was supposed to, partly because I wanted to. The kiss lasted and built up a small head of steam, and then she shuddered slightly and drew back.

"Damn it," she said, "I wish I were a call girl, Bill."

It would play either way. I kissed her again and felt the warmth and intensity of her embrace. I stroked the side of her face, let my hand trail lingeringly down the front of her fine body. Then I tensed up and let go of her and forced myself to step back. "I'll call you," I said softly. I let go of her hand and she turned into the house and closed the door and I went back to my place and tried to sleep.

It wasn't easy. I thought about two girls, a girl named Joyce and a girl named Barbara. I thought about two ways of life, a life of back rooms and fast action, a life of hard honest work and straight living. Dangerous thoughts for a man called Wizard.

I made more calls Wednesday, two to Murray's office, one to the Glade. I made them automatically, working like a programmed computer, speaking automatic words in my two mechanical fake voices. I left work early that day for my apartment. I took out the three onionskin copies I had typed up in Murray's office and read them through. The second one had Thursday's date at the top—tomorrow.

I took my Milani costume from the closet, spread it out on the bed. I looked at the snap-brim hat, the shabby suit, the loud and food-stained tie. I read through the letters again. Then I picked up the phone and dialed a number.

She answered it herself.

"Bill," I said.

"I've been wishing you would call," Joyce said. "I wanted to talk to you but I didn't know when it would be safe. How is it going, Wizard?"

"It's going all right."

"Tell me about it."

I lit a cigarette first. I took a deep drag, held the smoke in my lungs until I was slightly dizzy.

"Listen," I said.

She waited.

"I don't want to go through with it," I said. "I don't want to job the guy. I want to call it off."

10

"No," she said. "You're not going to do this to me, Wizard."

"Joyce—"

"You can't weasel out. It's all set up and we're going to push it through. You can't change your mind now," Joyce protested.

We weren't talking on the phone now. We had talked on the phone just long enough for her to be sure I wasn't kidding. Now we were in my living room and her Caddy was parked at the curb in front. She was standing in front of me and her eyes were angry. I asked her if she wanted a drink. She said she didn't. I made one for myself and she changed her mind and I made one for her. We sat at opposite ends of my living room couch and sipped scotch.

"Wizard?"

I met her gaze. She was angry now, and slightly desperate, and the combination of anger and desperation had deepened the lines at the corners of her mouth and pointed up the hardness of her face. And yet somehow her beauty was more striking than ever. My mind did what minds have a tendency to do, erected a little balance scale and put her on one side and Barb on the other. The contrast was vivid. Barb was soft and gentle, steady and sure, a good long-term investment. The other was fire and fury and handle-with-care, a much greater risk. And much more exciting.

"What changed your mind, Wizard? You were all ready to go, all set to job Murray and get the money and take me the hell out of this rotten town. What turned you off?"

"Things."

"What things?"

I finished my drink, started a cigarette. "A few things," I said. "In the first place, I don't think it would work. Murray is a highly respected guy. Clean, established. And on top of that he happens to be a lawyer. There are a million holes in the frame, Joyce. If he were someone shady it wouldn't matter, but a fellow like Murray could kick the prosecution's case to hell and back."

"You really don't think it would work?" Joyce said.

"That's right."

"I don't believe you, Wizard." Her eyes challenged me. I glanced down at my drink, which was gone. I dragged on my cigarette. I raised my eyes and she was still watching me. "I don't believe you at all," she said. "If you thought the frame was wrong you'd look for another way, a fresh angle. What's the real reason?"

I didn't answer her.

"You don't have to tell me," she said. "I can figure it out. You've had a taste of respectable life and you like the flavor. You're a salesman for Perry Carver. Or don't you call yourself a salesman? Maybe you prefer to think of yourself as an investment counselor."

"Joyce—"

"You play cards with the upper middle-class and you don't even cheat. You go out with a stinking schoolteacher—yes, I heard about your new love, honey. You go out with her and think about marriage and respectability and what a cushy little life it will be. Are you going to marry her, Wizard? Are you going to settle down in the suburbs like an All-American success story?"

I said, "Stop it."

"The hell I'll stop it! You're such a goddamned fool, Wizard. It's a kick now, isn't it? It was a kick for me, too. I didn't just marry Murray for his money. I wanted a house with a lawn and a backyard. I wanted people to look at me without wetting their lips and wondering how much it would cost. Oh, it's fine for the first little while. It's a brand-new way to live. But it changes. It turns sour. It gets so damned dull you could scream.

"It doesn't work, Wizard. It doesn't work because it's a lie, a stupid lie front to back. You wind up wasting your life on a bunch of fatheaded squares who don't speak your language or think your thoughts. You shape yourself over and try to convince yourself you've managed to change inside, and then one day you wake up and realize you never changed at all and you're a very round peg stuck in the squarest hole on earth. Your little schoolteacher won't be much fun then. Your little job will be the biggest bore since Maynard the Magnificent. And if you think I'm going to let you blow a damned good chance for both of us you've got to be out of your mind."

There was more. It went on like that, and I sat there telling her she was wrong and trying to make myself believe it. Maybe the good life hadn't worked for her. It could still work for me. I had floated into the gray world of the card mechanic pretty much by accident, and I could float out just as easily and just as accidentally. I didn't feel that much of a commitment to dishonesty.

But she had another argument, and it was more persuasive. She stood up and planted herself in front of me, and before she delivered it she put her hands at the sides of her breasts and ran them slowly down the length of her body. Then she grinned at me.

"You can't get out," she said.

"Why not?"

"Because I'll damn well ruin you. Do you think Perry Carver would keep a crook on his payroll? Do you think Sy and Murray and the others would want a card sharp in their game? And they would find out, Wizard. I'd make sure they found out. Your new friends wouldn't have any use for you. Neither would your new little lost love. Are you laying that schoolteacher, Wizard?"

I didn't mean to slap her. My hand moved by itself, rising fast and landing over her left cheekbone. She reeled backward and for a moment I thought she was going to fall over. But she only smiled.

"You can have the teacher," Joyce said levelly. "You can keep your job. Some day you'll wake up, but you can sleep as long as you want, if that's the way you want it. But first you're going to take care of Murray for me."

She didn't wait for an answer. She turned on her heel and stamped out of my apartment, hopped into her car, took off fast enough to leave a rubber patch on the street outside.

It must have been around five-thirty when Joyce left. I had a few drinks after that. I went out for a bite, ate a third of a hamburger and left the rest. It didn't taste right. I don't suppose there was anything wrong with the hamburger. It just didn't taste right.

So I went back to my place and had a few more drinks and I stared at the onionskin letters some more and looked at the Milani costume. I squinted at myself in the mirror, too. But not for very long.

And then I called Joyce. She must have been sitting on top of the phone because she picked it up before the first ring was finished.

I said, "All right. I'm in."

"Of course," she said. "Because there's no way out."

I called Murray's office at nine o'clock the next evening. There was no answer. I let it ring long enough to make sure that no one had stuck around. Then I drove to the Rand Building on the double. I followed the established routine—I took the elevator to the seventeenth floor and walked the rest of the way. I let myself into his office, thumbed through the Yellow Pages, found a twenty-four hour messenger service. I called them and told them to send a kid over for a pick-up and delivery.

During the day I had picked up a batch of singles from the bank, along with a couple hundreds. While the kid was on his way over I made a bundle of money, a sheaf of singles with two one-hundreds at the top and bottom of the roll. I stuffed the money into an envelope and started to scrawl A. Milani on it. Then I changed my mind and typed the name on Murray's office typewriter. I sealed the envelope and dropped it on the table in the outer office. I left the hall door open and retired to Murray's private office and sat in his chair, with the door closed.

When the kid came in I called to him through the

closed door. "There's an envelope on the table there," I said. "Run it over to the Hotel Glade near the station. It's for a man named August Milani. Make sure you give it to him in person."

I had left a five-spot on the table along with the envelope. I told the kid to help himself to it. As soon as he left I whistled the hell out of Murray's office, ran down seven flights of stairs and caught an elevator the rest of the way. I drove home, changed into my Milani costume, hurried over to the Glade. I made myself slow down on the way in, forced myself to walk with the head-back, shoulders-slouched swagger of my man Milani.

The kid was there when I reached the hotel. He leaned up against the desk, waiting to deliver Milani's envelope in person. I took it from him, gave him a quarter and watched him go. Then I turned to the desk clerk, a buddy by now—I'd been cultivating him carefully. I winked at him, then ripped open the envelope and snatched up the stack of bills. His eyes bugged.

"Money," I said.

I fanned the bills for him. He saw the hundreds on the top and the hundreds on the bottom, and all the singles in the middle were just a big flash of green ink.

"Money," I said again.

And I started dealing the bills out, slapping them one after the other onto the top of the counter. The basic principle is pretty much the same as the one used in a second deal or a bottom deal. Each time I was slapping down two bills, a hundred on top and a single under it. Each time fast fingerwork brought the hundred back on to the top of the stack for the next shot. By the time I was finished there wasn't any question in the desk clerk's mind. Quite obviously I had a stack of hundred-dollar bills.

"Jesus," he said.

"I told you, didn't I? I leave this town in the longest Caddy Detroit ever made."

"How did you get that kind of dough?" the clerk said.

I winked at him. "A guy named Rogers," I said. "The one who left me all them nasty messages."

"Yeah?"

I nodded solemnly. "Yeah," I said. "Can you keep a secret?"

"Sure."

"So can I." I laughed aloud. "And that's where all this wonderful bread came from. I get paid for keeping secrets. I get paid real nice."

"What did he do?"

"Who?"

"Rogers," the clerk said. I was glad to see he could remember the name. "What the hell did he do?"

"Nothing."

"But—"

"He's a real nice guy," I said. "A big-time lawyer. It's

just that he's got this little secret, see? And he'll pay to keep it."

I slapped the roll of bills against the palm of my hand. "And I'll tell you a secret," I said. "He ain't done paying yet. That bastard just started."

I left him there and went to my room at the rear of the hotel. I closed the door, locked it. I tucked the bills into my pocket, dropped the envelope on the floor in a corner of the room. The envelope had Murray Rogers' return address on it. It would probably still be there in the room on Monday, since the personnel at the Glade weren't too fanatic about housekeeping.

The window stuck the first time I tried it. I worked on it, got it open. The courtyard in back was littered with trash and broken wine bottles. In the back of the courtyard there was a driveway that ran through to Tupper on the other side of the block. I closed the window. I tried it again, and this time it opened easily. It would open as easily on Monday.

Monday.

Monday was going to be an important day. The last letter on Murray's typewriter had Monday's date on top. And Monday was the day when I would wear the shabby suit and the snap-brim hat for the final time.

August Milani was going to die on Monday. Murray Rogers was going to kill him.

11

Friday I sold a unit and a half of our current syndication during the morning without leaving my desk. I had a lazy lunch in the Panmore Men's Grill with Jack Kimball, another of Perry's salesmen. We ate Welsh rarebits and drank Dutch beer and talked shop for two hours. I spent the afternoon looking over some brochures on new syndicates Perry was thinking about handling. There was a bowling alley in Baltimore with a fifteen percent payout, a shopping center in New Rochelle, a St. Louis apartment house. I thought the shopping center offered the safest return and would be the easiest to push, and I typed up a memo to Perry with my recommendation. At five o'clock he handed me a check for my commissions on sales to date. Even with the five-hundred buck advance chopped off, the sum was a decent amount. I won money at the poker game that night. We played at Ed Hart's place in a downstairs game room similar to Murray's. I wound up eighty bucks ahead, mostly by honest play with a few assists from sleight-of-hand. The cheating, such as it was, was almost automatic. Like the palmed-off five spot at the lunch counter a week or so earlier. That sort of habit is a hard one to break. I played fairly well and the cards ran my way, so even without a little of the best of it I would have cleared fifty bucks or so. The cheating was worth the extra thirty to me.

Saturday I slept late, soaked in a tub, cracked a fresh fifth of scotch, drove around town aimlessly, took Barb to dinner. We wound up going to a movie, finally. I held her hand through the show, and now and then she gave me a little squeeze.

Would I hold hands with Joyce? No, of course not. We might leave the movie in a hurry and find a hotel room. We might watch the movie all the way through without any contact at all. But we would never sit holding hands in a theater balcony.

We were too damned hip for that.

After the show I suggested going some place and drinking. Barb said she had scotch at her place. "The seats are comfortable and the privacy can't be beat," she said. "And the prices are eminently reasonable, Bill."

So at her house we sat on her couch and drank her scotch out of coffee mugs because she couldn't find appropriate glasses. We pretended it was Prohibition and we were in a subtle speakeasy. She did a terrible imitation of Walter Winchell announcing *The Untouchables,* and I poured fresh scotch into our cups, and we put Ella Fitzgerald records on the player.

I don't remember who suggested dancing. We wound up giving it a whirl. I held her a little closer than necessary and clomped around ponderously and tried to remember how long it had been since I'd done any dancing. That had been a big thing with Carole before we had been married. After the marriage had ended I didn't have anyone to dance with. A card sharp doesn't take his girls dancing or dance with them in a living room. He lets them lose his money on the dogs or the horses, takes them to hip parties or clip-joint nightclubs, and once in their apartments he beds them down as soon as possible. But I was dancing with Barbara now, and I was enjoying it.

I kept enjoying it more. Barb's cheek stayed next to mine. Her perfume was subtle but distinctive, a fresh, cutely sexy scent. I held her close and felt her breasts press against my chest. My arm was around her waist. Somewhere along the way my arm moved a few inches lower and pressed her flanks. They were marvelous. I drew her close and felt the warmth of her loins. She began breathing a little harder. I kissed her and she purred.

We continued dancing. I stroked her and she danced with delicious little hip motions that racked her loins against mine and had the right effect on both of us. I wanted her with a sweet tender ache that improved as it developed. There was no urgency, just the sure feeling that sooner or later the record would end and I would have this girl and she would be divine.

The record ended. The player shut itself off. I still held her and I still stroked her and she still made those delicious movements with her delicious hips, but we were not dancing any more. We slipped into her bedroom, and we took off all our clothes and put them neatly aside, and we rolled into bed.

Her flesh was sweet and yielding. We took a long time loving each other. I touched all of her body, marveling over her beauty, and each caress pitched her passion higher. I kissed her breasts, teased them with my tongue. I found her with my fingers and she shivered and quivered and surged with delight.

I sought her and found her and we were together and she moaned and she held me. We rocked together and the whole earth sang.

Afterward Barbara cried a little, giggled a little, said that maybe she was a call girl after all, then cried some more. I drew her close and told her that everything was all right. She rolled on to her side, supporting her weight on an elbow, and looked at me.

"It's been so long," she said

"Barb—"

"So very long..."

I returned to my apartment and took a bottle to bed with me. The next day I didn't do much of anything. I spoke to a few people on the phone—Barb, Joyce, Sy

Daniels. I put in an appearance at the Glade and wound up spending the night there. Early Monday morning I left, changed clothes at my apartment, and went to the office.

It was a dull day. Then it was night, and time to work.

I stuck around the Black Sand office until Murray left. Then I carried the three onionskin copies upstairs to his office and tucked them away in a file drawer under M for Milani. I made it out of there on the double and dropped the duplicate key into a sewer. I didn't need it anymore.

After dinner I headed for my room at the Glade and waited for the desk clerk to go across the street and return. He made the trip every evening around eight—ducked across to the Silver Dollar and had a shot and a beer, sometimes a few extra shots if he felt like it. He was a quickie drinker, but it still took him fifteen or twenty minutes and the desk was untended during that time. This time he left at five to eight and stayed away for half an hour.

Murray was home alone. Joyce had taken the younger daughter shopping and the older one had a date.

When the clerk was back behind the desk everything was ready. I rolled up my left sleeve, took a penknife from my pocket, killed the germs on the blade with my cigarette lighter flame and made a good gash halfway up my forearm. It took me three tries before I could force myself to make the cut. I sprang a blood vessel or two and started bleeding. I bled on the bed, dripped beads of blood onto the floor. After a few seconds I opened up a band-aid and slapped it on the cut.

Then I took a pair of hundreds from my wallet. I opened up the dresser drawer, dropped the bills on top of a flashy sport shirt and left the drawer open. After the way I had flashed money at the clerk, robbery might look like a possible motive. With money lying around like this, the cops could cross robbery off their list.

I flipped the hat on the floor, caved in the crown with my foot. I dropped the drugstore eyeglasses and stepped on them hard enough to break both lenses. I put the frames in a pocket for the time being.

My arm was beginning to throb a little. I gave a check to see if the cut were bleeding through the band-aid. No blood.

There was a glass ashtray on the little table next to the bed. I knocked it to the floor. The damned thing bounced around crazily without breaking and wound up somewhere under the bed. I dug out the receptacle and tried again. It shattered.

I picked the phone off the hook, set it down. The desk clerk started babbling hello at nobody in particular. There was a fifty-nine cent cap pistol in my pocket, a recent purchase from a notions store. I took out the pistol and squeezed the trigger. It made a nice noise, left a gunpowder smell hanging in the air. Then I picked up the telephone, and the voice I used was Murray Rogers.

"It's nothing," I said. "Just knocked the phone off the hook, that's all. Forget it."

I hung up before he could think it over. In a minute or two, if he had half a brain, he would put two and two together and deliver the desired five. I took a quick breath, then tugged the pillowcase off the pillow the management had stuck at the head of the bed. I used the pillowcase to wipe up some of the blood from the floor. Then I threw open the window and dropped down into the courtyard.

I had the pillowcase in a pocket, the hat and eyeglass frames in one hand. I tossed the hat to the ground, flipped the frames near it. The next step hurt like hell. I yanked off the band-aid, opened up the cut on my forearm and left a trail of blood leading away from the window toward the rear of the courtyard. Then I re-fastened the band-aid over the gash and took off my jacket and dragged it along the ground for twenty or thirty yards. I put on the jacket again and got the hell out of there. I didn't run. I walked quickly to the back of the courtyard and out through the driveway. So far as I could determine, nobody had observed me.

My car was parked at the curb. I drove away from the neighborhood as fast as you can drive without risking a ticket. When I reached Murray's house, I parked a few doors down the street. I hurried up his driveway to the rear of the house, opened a gun-metal garbage can, stuffed the bloody pillowcase into it. I put the lid on, clambered into the car and headed for my apartment.

I didn't start to shake until I was inside my apartment with the door shut. Then my hands trembled and my heart pretended it was a triphammer. I poured a shot of scotch and spilled half of it on the way to my mouth. The second shot steadied me.

The cut on my arm had opened up again. The blood had soaked through the band-aid to the shirt and through the shirt to the jacket. That didn't matter. I wouldn't have much use for shirt or jacket again.

I tried to make sure of the cut now. I washed it out with scotch since it had a higher alcohol content than anything else in the house, and then I fixed up the wound with a gauze pad and a few strips of adhesive.

The Broadway suit and the shirt and the loud tie all were dumped into the incinerator. There would be traces there—buttons that didn't burn, things like that. That wouldn't much matter. The police wouldn't be looking in my incinerator for Milani's clothing. The police would be looking for Milani himself, for one thing, and they wouldn't have any interest in one William Maynard to begin with. The shoes I put into the closet along with the little cap pistol. In a day or two I would flip them into a trash barrel somewhere.

I poured another drink and tossed it off. The gash in my arm felt better now, either because the cut was healing or because the liquor was anesthetizing it. I sat down on the couch and turned on the radio, dialing in a station that gave you music and spot news twenty-four hours a day. There was a news flash at nine but it had nothing about Milani.

The hell—the plan couldn't really miss now. The stage was set perfectly. The desk clerk at the Glade would tell the cops about a seedy criminal type from Brooklyn named August Milani who had acted as though he were going to come into a fortune, who did come into the fortune, and who told the clerk that he, Milani, made the fortune by keeping a secret for a lawyer named Murray Rogers. The cops would tooth-comb Milani's room and find the aftermath of a murder. Room knocked around, bloodstains, a broken ashtray, shattered eyeglass lenses, the faint smell of gunpowder. The desk clerk would admit he had been away for half an hour or so, obviously the logical time for Rogers to move in on the scene.

And there would be plenty more. Rogers' receptionist would tell the police about a nasty-voiced man who had kept trying to talk to Rogers, and Murray would try to explain that the man had been some nutty insurance salesman. The authorities would find the letters in the Rogers file. Murray would deny writing them. The authorities would find the bloody pillowcase in the Rogers garbage can, and the blood would match the stains in Milani's hotel room. Murray would say he didn't know how the pillowcase had found its way into the garbage can. The police would ask Murray who Whitlock was and what hold Milani had over him. Murray Rogers couldn't tell the police because he wouldn't know anything about Whitlock or a "hold." The authorities would keep on asking and Murray would never be able to come up with the answers.

The desk clerk would remember the messenger. The messenger would tell the cops he picked up a bundle at Murray's office and gave it to Milani in person. Murray would say he didn't know anything about it. The police would ask him what he did with Milani's body and he would try to make them believe he never met any Milani, that Milani was just a persistent voice on the telephone.

Murray Rogers, the poor bastard, didn't have a chance.

I caught a news flash at nine-thirty. A man had been assaulted or possibly murdered at a downtown hotel. Police were working on the case and had several good leads. They expected to wrap it up quickly. No names were mentioned, but the confidence was obvious. The cops had this one in the bag already and they didn't care who knew it.

I sat there and listened to more music and wondered what was going to go wrong. Something had to go wrong. This wasn't a deal off a stacked deck in a bust-out joint. This was a big one. One little snag somewhere along the way would blow the works to hell and back.

The telephone rang at ten minutes of ten like a small bomb and the noise shattered the comparative silence of the apartment. I reached over, switched off the radio. I picked up the receiver and held it to my ear.

Her voice was music.

"It worked," she said.

"What happened?"

"It worked like a charm. The cops just left and they took Murray along with them. I didn't hear much of it. They asked him if he knew anybody named Milani. He said he didn't. They asked again and he said that Milani was some insurance salesman but he had never met the man."

"And?"

"And they zipped him up and took him to jail," she said. "I have to hang up now. He wanted me to call his lawyer, but I decided to call you first."

I didn't say anything. I felt numb now. The scheme had worked so far, it was going nicely, and I didn't know whether to laugh or to cry.

"Darling?" A soft chuckle. "You're a wizard, darling. You really are."

12

From there on, it was everybody's ball game. The whole town was busy for the next ten days. Murray found himself the best criminal lawyer in town, a man named Nester who handled most of the important cases in the area. He had two sets of clients—rich men in trouble, and hoods. Murray was a rich man, and he was sure as hell in trouble.

He hired Nester. Murray also hired the local agency of a national detective outfit. He drove the lawyer and the detectives out of their minds. According to what I learned through Joyce, both Nester and the detectives took it for granted that Murray was guilty. All Nester did was try to persuade Murray to level so a way could be found to break the case. Murray kept on shouting that it was all crazy, that some bastard was framing him. And the more the detectives dug around, the guiltier Murray appeared.

The district attorney was digging around, too. It was a colorful case—wealthy killer, shocked and pretty young wife, and enough elements of mystery to give the theory-builders a kick or two. The newspapers gave it a big play, one daily screaming for Murray's head, and the other staying more on the solemn side.

It was the sort of case that a politically ambitious district attorney would be well advised to win. This public prosecutor was ambitious as hell.

Every joker had a different notion. Somebody suggested that Milani hadn't been killed, that he was wounded and was biding his time in a gangland hideout, ready to wreak revenge on Murray as soon as he was released. Other geniuses insisted that Rogers hadn't done the job himself at all, that he had hired professionals and that Milani was in the river wearing a cement overcoat. The music went round and round, and I sat back and tried not to listen.

The grand jury was to meet on Thursday, ten days after the arrest had been made. I was out with Barb Lambert Wednesday night. We had dinner and then went over to her place for records and conversation, and I was in a mood. She misread it as concern for a close friend. She asked me what would happen to Murray Rogers.

"I don't know," I said.

"Will he—"

"Go to the electric chair?" I said.

She shuddered.

"No," I said. "There's not much chance of that. The prosecution has a good case, but the evidence is all circumstantial. It's probably enough to send him to prison, but not enough to—to hang him. Or electrocute him."

"But how can they call it murder? Don't they need a corpus delicti?"

"They've got that."

"You mean Milani's body was found?"

"You don't need a body for corpus delicti. All corpus delicti means is evidence that a particular crime was committed. And there's plenty of that, body or no body."

There was enough for the grand jury to return an indictment, at any rate. I was in the courtroom for the hearing, along with Joyce and a few of Murray's other friends. The prosecution's case sounded even more damning in a courtroom with a judge and jury and batteries of lawyers on either side.

If Murray had actually been guilty, he might have been in a position to make a better case for himself. By telling how Milani had been blackmailing him and bleeding him white, Murray could have built up a lot of sympathy, and by a little legal footwork he could have had the charge reduced all the way down to manslaughter, with a possible bid for temporary insanity or self-defense, the two traditional refuges for the accused having committed murder with extenuating circumstances.

But Murray couldn't take any refuges even if he had wanted to. He couldn't tell them what Milani had been blackmailing him for. Murray couldn't locate the corpse. He could only stammer and scream about a frameup.

And nobody was listening.

The outcome was never really in doubt. The jury indicted Murray Rogers for murder in the first degree. The offense is not a bailable one. I sat there and watched the guards take him away, shoulders slumped and face drawn and eyes vacant. He passed a few feet from me and didn't seem to see me at all. It was just as well. I couldn't have met his eyes.

Friday night.

I sat in my bedroom alone and did card tricks in front of a mirror. My hands weren't too nimble because I was tight. The bottle of Cutty Sark was on the dresser. Every now and then I took a swig and the whiskey went right down without my tasting it at all.

During the days I had been a machine. I had made the motions at the office, and the motions when I took prospects out to lunch or met them at their homes. Nothing had seemed to reach me. Once I had spent an hour with a prospect, had talked at length about everything under the sun, and had wound up selling him a nice bundle. And when I had left him and returned to the office to type out some forms, I hadn't been able to remember his name. Everything had been automatic, mechanical, and nothing had made any impression at all.

The nights had been a little different. The nights had been solo ventures for the most part, with Barb on hand now and then, more often than I wanted her and less often than she would have preferred it. It had been funny because I was clear now. Joyce had let me off the hook, and I could court Barb and marry her if I wanted to. But things had changed since Murray's arrest. Something very significant had taken place, and Barb's version of what had happened did not mesh with mine because she did not know what I had done. And I couldn't tell her.

Which had made a difference. The little middle-class nook that had seemed so desirable included a wife with whom you could discuss everything—excluding your semi-annual infidelities, at least. And the more bits and pieces there were that I could not possibly tell Barb about, the less I could imagine myself spending the rest of my life with her.

So we had cooled off a little. I had never shared her bed after that one night. She hadn't asked why. She may have written it off as mood, or she may have decided that I was an intensely moral person. Whatever, I had been spending most of the nights alone—after Murray's arrest and indictment.

But the night had been rarely spent sober. I had become blind drunk only once. That had been on the night after the indictment had been returned, and that night I had wound up getting tossed out of a wino hangout on Skid Row and crawling in the gutter while my insides had spilled out. Most of the time I had just put a heavy edge on and sat around thinking. Maybe I was drinking to keep from dreaming, because without a good skinful I had some dreams that woke me up sweating and panting.

The hell with it.

It was Friday night, and I was doing card tricks poorly in front of a mirror, and I was about half in the bag, and the phone rang. I put down the cards and answered.

It was Joyce.

"You weren't supposed to call," I said. "We aren't supposed to get in touch with each other."

"I know."

"So what's it all about?"

"I have to see you, Wizard. There are some things I have to talk about with you."

"Go ahead."

"Not on the phone. In person."

"I don't like it," I said. "It's no good if people see us together, find out we're spending any time with each other. We're not airtight, you know. All they have to do is start checking me and the fat's in every fire in town."

"You mean your background?" Joyce said.

"To hell with my background. Give that clerk at the Glade two looks at me and he'll recognize me as Milani. We're safe as long as they don't check us. That's all."

"I know," Joyce said. "But there's nothing suspicious

about a man's good friend coming to see his wife in her hour of need. Sy and Harold were over yesterday. It would look even worse if you don't come, you know. As though we were staying apart for a reason."

That made strong sense. I straightened up my clothes and combed my hair. I hurried the Ford over to her house and parked in front. She opened the door before I could hit the bell. I started to say something but she motioned me inside, shut the door. She didn't look good. Her face was drawn and her eyes were a little bloodshot, as though she had been drinking or as though she hadn't slept much lately.

"Why, Bill," she said. "It's—nice of you to come. Can I get you anything to drink?"

There was a girl curled up in an armchair in front the television set. She was reading a book and ignoring the set. She glanced up at us and smiled.

"You've met Jenny," Joyce said, "haven't you?"

"I don't believe I have."

Joyce introduced me to the girl. Jenny was about seventeen, dark-haired and pretty. She had Murray's features but they were softer on the female model.

"Daddy used to talk about you all the time, Mr. Maynard," she said. "Gee, isn't it awful?"

"It certainly is."

She stood up from the chair, shaking her head bitterly. "Somebody must have framed Daddy," she said. "Don't you think so?"

"I guess so," I said.

Her face clouded. "Because he couldn't have—couldn't have—killed somebody—"

She stopped talking. Her eyes closed, blinked, opened. She forced a smile to her lips, then shrugged her narrow shoulders. "I'll let you and Joyce talk, Mr. Maynard. It's been very nice meeting you."

We stood there, silent, while she dejectedly quit the room. Her bedroom door closed with a bang. Joyce was shaking now and her eyes kept darting around aimlessly. I put a hand on her shoulder to steady her and she sagged against me, limp as a eunuch. I caught her, made her sit down.

"There's a bottle of scotch in the bar," she said, pointing. "I need some."

"Ice?"

"Just scotch in a glass."

I poured scotch into a glass and took it over to her. Joyce drank off half of it and put the glass down on the coffee table. I gave her a cigarette, lit it for her. She took two drags. Then she had some more of the scotch.

I said, "What's it all about?"

"He's coming home, Bill."

"Murray?"

"Yes."

"But—"

"His lawyer, Nester, was over here a few hours ago,"

she said. "He was very pleased with himself. He managed to make a deal with the district attorney. The charge is being reduced to second-degree murder and Murray will be out on bail by Monday morning."

"He's copping a plea?"

"Not exactly. Murray will plead guilty by reason of temporary insanity. There will still be a trial. Nester thinks he can win it."

I lit a cigarette. "I don't understand," I said. "It doesn't make any sense."

"I know."

"Because he can't plead guilty, damn it! He can't tell what tax fraud he's guilty of and he can't explain what he did with Milani's body. I don't get it at all."

"That's why I'm worried, Wizard."

She started to say something else, then stopped short. A door opened somewhere in the rear of the house. We listened to footsteps, and Jenny stepped into the room. She looked as though she had been crying, but she had herself under control now. She had changed to a black skirt and sweater and she had a book under her arm.

"I was thinking of going out for a little while," she said. "You don't mind, do you, Joyce?"

Joyce said she didn't mind. The girl said goodbye to us and left. I thought how hard it must have been on her. Her circle would be giving her a rough time now. And everything would be just wild confusion, a parade of frightening events that could make no sense at all to her.

"Wizard? I don't think he's going to plead guilty."

"What do you mean?"

"I know Murray," she said. "I think he went along with Nester because he wanted to get out of jail. Murray can't expect to get by with a plea without answering a lot of questions that he can't answer. I think he's got something planned."

"Like what?"

"I don't know. He might want to leave the country. He's not young, you know. Even if he got off with a few years in jail, that would be too much for him. I don't think he'd be willing to settle for even a short prison sentence."

"Where would he go?"

"South America, probably. You can buy citizenship down there if you have the money. And he could raise the money in a day. He could get out of jail on Monday and catch a plane Tuesday."

She knew him better than I did. Maybe she was right. Maybe he would run like that, make a quick dash for freedom. It didn't seem too logical to me, didn't seem in character with what I knew of Murray. And yet he was in a bind—maybe running was the only way open.

"Suppose he does that," Joyce said. "Where does that leave me?"

"Sitting pretty."

"Why?"

"Because when you divorce a fugitive you get every cent he has."

She shook her head impatiently. "You don't understand. He'll want me to go with him, me and the girls. I don't want to spend my life with him in Brazil."

"You might like Brazil, Joyce."

"Damn it—"

"Easy," I said. "It's no problem. You tell him to go by himself. He travels faster who travels alone, that old bit. You can always join him later. They can't hold you, you know. Once he's out of the country, you just forget about joining him. It's that simple."

She didn't answer me. There was something on her mind that struck deeper than her husband's possible plans for leaving the country. I sat down next to her, took hold of her shoulder.

"All right," I said. "Tell me what it's all about."

"It's nothing."

"Give, Joyce."

"He's having me followed," she said.

The rest of it was blurted out. Men had been following her, she was sure; men had been watching the house and keeping tabs on her, and she was so worried she thought she was going to go out of her mind.

So maybe he wasn't going to Brazil, I thought. Maybe he wanted to get out on bail so that he could do a little spadework on his own. Maybe he had it all figured out already and he was coming home to wring her neck for her.

And maybe he had me tied into the picture, as far as that went. Hell, if he were thinking it out, he would hit the possibility of my involvement sooner or later. Everything connected with Milani started after my arrival in town. He might not write that off as coincidence. He might put two and two together until he came up with something.

I tried to remember if anyone had been following me lately. If they had been, I hadn't noticed them—not that I had been looking too hard. But I hadn't done anything suspicious. I was clear enough.

"Listen," I told her. "It's only natural, for God's sake. You and I and Murray are the only ones in the world who know he's being framed. You and I know because we did it. He knows because it was done to him. He's going to be suspicious all over the place. He may have you tailed, but nobody can dig up anything that will make you look bad. Don't worry about it."

"I can't help worrying, Wizard."

I thought quickly. "He's coming home Monday," I said. "Tomorrow is Saturday. Can he have visitors?"

"Of course. I see him once a day."

"Could I see him?"

"Certainly. I'm surprised you haven't gone already. His other friends have been there. Most of them, anyway."

"I think I'll go, then. Tomorrow afternoon, say. I should be able to draw him out a little and find out what he's planned. At least I can find out whether or not we've got anything to worry about."

That seemed to reassure her a little. She asked me to make fresh drinks. I told her no, that if the house were being watched, it wouldn't look good if I stuck around too long. A sympathy call was fine, but you couldn't extend it for too long a period.

She came to me, wanting to be kissed. I didn't want to kiss her. But she pressed herself against me and my arms circled her and our mouths met.

It was funny. I didn't even like her anymore. She was my partner in a crime I was not proud of. I didn't want to have anything to do with her. I wanted to finish things up, tie the ends neatly and never see her again.

But the electrical impulses still worked. The contact set us off again. Just as the contact had always done, and animal need came on like gangbusters. I fought with myself. And, for a change, I won. I pushed her away and left and strode quickly to the Ford. Once behind the wheel, I started the engine and pulled away. There were no cars with people in them parked on the block. If Murray were having her watched, it wasn't on an around-the-clock basis.

Did Murray really suspect anything? I didn't want to think about it. Joyce and I had one of those set-ups that was perfect until someone started to pick at it. As soon as anyone suspected us, we were through.

It was easier to agree that Murray was ready to run for Brazil, or that he was resigned to going to jail for the shortest time possible. I hoped Brazil was his answer. Jail would be bad for him. And despite all my previous attempts, I couldn't make myself hate the guy, couldn't even dislike him a little—even though he had irritated me with his smugness to begin with.

But it's no fun jobbing someone who has helped you. With luck you can make yourself despise your mark long enough to con him and get him out of the way.

But now the reverse was happening. The further the scene developed, the more I liked Murray Rogers.

And the less I liked myself.

13

They were holding Murray Rogers at the city jail along with the drunks and the sex criminals. I drove down there shortly after noon. The jail was a bulky old building, a massive structure as inviting as a Gothic novel. I walked up a flight of high stone steps and opened a heavy door. There was a big cop behind the desk. I told him who I was and what I wanted and he nodded. He called a guard and relayed the information to him, and the guard led me up creaking wooden stairs to the second floor.

We walked down a long hallway. Most of the cells were clean and modern, but most of the inmates were last night's drunks and they had spent the night puking on their shoes. In one cell a man was singing *Molly Malone* in a whiskey tenor. In another cell an older man was hawking and spitting.

Murray Rogers was all the way down at the end of the corridor. The guard and I stopped in front of his cell and he looked at us, his face breaking into a smile when he saw me.

"Bill," he said hoarsely, "I've been waiting for you to drop around. How's it going?"

I said something pleasant. The guard opened the

cell door with a key and locked me inside with Murray. "Ten minutes," he said. "That's all I can give you, Mr. Maynard."

The guard left. Murray rose to his feet, pumped my hand enthusiastically. He had made a rather dramatic recovery since the day of the indictment. His handshake was firm and his face had its color back again.

"Sit down," he said. "This little hole isn't much, but it's comfortable enough. And I'll be out of here Monday."

"Joyce told me."

"You've seen her?"

"Last night."

"Poor kid," he said. "It's been hell for her, Bill. And for the girls. But I think the worst of it is over. The suddenness shocked them all, but you'd be surprised how much a human being can stand once he or she learns to accept it." He waved his hands at the cell. "This, for example. I was going stir-crazy, Bill. I was in a state of traumatic shock and all I could think about was that I wanted to be free again. I denied everything, of course. I couldn't explain all their evidence, and I just denied it."

He offered me a cigar. I shook my head and he unwrapped one for himself and bit off the tip. "They won't let me have a cigar cutter," he said. "Afraid I'll open my veins with it. The damned fools."

I gave him a light. He blew out a cloud of smoke and

winked at me through it. "I gave Nester a hell of a time at first," he said. "I kept denying everything like an idiot. Now I've always felt that any man who can't play straight with his own lawyer isn't worth the powder to blow him to hell. You know, when you're established and respected and well-to-do, you can't believe you could ever get in legal trouble. The mind refuses to accept it. But the indictment did something to me. You were at the grand jury session, weren't you?"

I nodded.

"Well, that was the turning point. That day in court damn near killed me, Bill. Knocked me for a loop. So Thursday night and Friday morning I did a lot of careful thinking. And when Alex Nester came in to see me I leveled with him finally. I told him there was no sense playing games any more. I killed Milani. Now all he had to do was get me off."

I was sitting on the edge of his army cot. Murray was next to me. When he finished his last three sentences I almost fell off the cot. My face must have changed expression. That much was all right—it was okay to be surprised, but I couldn't let myself be incredulous.

I said, "Then you did kill him?"

"Of course I did. What did you think, Bill?"

"I believed you."

"That it was all a frameup? I suppose you and Joyce were the only people in the world who did believe me, then. Maybe a few other close friends who couldn't imagine me being capable of murder. That's nonsense. There isn't a man in creation who isn't capable of murder once you give him the means and motive and opportunity. I'm hardly the murderous type, Bill, but I killed August Milani as sure as God made little green apples. I didn't have much choice. My back was up against the wall."

I managed to light a cigarette.

There were a few possibilities that occurred to me. Maybe Murray was crazy—maybe by now he managed to believe that he had killed Milani, that everyone else was right about it and Murray was wrong. Or else he was going for the safe play, hedging his bet by copping the plea and trying for a temporary insanity defense. I asked him if he wanted to tell me about it.

"Nothing much to tell," he said. "I was a party to a very large case of tax evasion. It involved a couple of real estate deals, and the end result was that the government got screwed out of close to two million dollars in income taxes. Milani knew about it, God knows how. He had proof. He could reach the Internal Revenue boys and make things very rough for us. What I did was out-and-out criminal, Bill. It meant a heavy fine and a jail sentence no matter how you looked at it."

"I see."

"So Milani tried blackmailing me," Murray continued. "I tried to dodge him but he had me over a barrel. Finally I paid him off, sent the money over to his hotel. He was greedy. He had a perfect fish on his hook and he wasn't going to stop with one payment. On Monday I went to see him. I was just going to argue with him, try to make him see I couldn't afford to contribute to a private fund for the enrichment of August Milani for the rest of my life. I had no intention of killing him. It happened by itself, or at least it seemed to. We started arguing. I grabbed him by the throat. He pulled a gun on me. I took it away from him and—I shot him."

He said all this very sincerely, very convincingly. If I hadn't known better I would have believed him without thinking twice about it.

"The body," I said. "What did you do with it?"

"Dragged it through the alley, stuffed it into my car and drove to the lake shore. I stuffed his clothing with rocks and lead pipe and tossed him in. I barely remember that part. I was in a fog from the moment I shot him. Everything's very fuzzy. I meant to throw the pillowcase in with him but I forgot. So I wound up stuffing it in my own garbage can."

"And the gun?"

"In the lake."

I dropped my cigarette on the floor, covered it with my shoe. "Jesus," I said. "What happens to you now?"

"I don't know, Bill. At the worst they'll call it manslaughter of one degree or another. With luck it will go as temporary insanity—that's what we're trying for. Nester's a good man. He says we have about a sixty percent chance of getting off scot-free."

"And the tax evasion?"

"No problem there," he said. "I could tell the Treasury Department agents about it, but I don't intend to. And they can't force me, because I can always take the fifth amendment to avoid incriminating myself. Milani had information, but Milani is dead now."

"Can they trace him?"

"Evidently not. The police have been trying, naturally. Milani probably isn't even his right name. They can't find any record of a man by that name and they couldn't lift any fingerprints from the room at the Glade. The police know I was mixed up in something very crooked but they don't have a case until they know something about it. And they'll never find out a thing. I won't tell them, my associates won't tell them, and Milani can't tell them."

"Then you're in pretty good shape," I said.

"It could be a lot worse, Bill."

"How do you feel about it?"

He stood up, paced the floor with his hands clasped behind his back. "Not so good and not so bad," he said slowly. "I was a wreck at first. The whole concept of murder—well, it gets to you. Were you in combat?"

"No."

"Neither was I. I was just old enough to go into a defense plant during the Second World War. Later on I did government tax work. I suppose it would be different for someone who saw combat, someone who killed men in the line of duty. But I never killed anyone before Milani, never witnessed a violent death. The idea of homicide took a little getting used to. I'm used to it now."

"Uh-huh."

He sighed. "It means a change in my living pattern," he went on. "I've got the mark of Cain now. I don't imagine we can go on living in this town, not very comfortably." He smiled softly. "Maybe we'll travel, Bill. Joyce has always wanted to travel, though she's never pressed the point. I think she feels cramped in a town like this one. She's used to a more sophisticated environment. I can afford to retire. Maybe we'll try traveling until everything cools off."

Our ten minutes were up, and with interest. The guard came back, an apologetic look on his face, and told me I'd have to be going now. I shook hands with Murray and he pumped my arm.

"It's funny," he said. "I couldn't tell this to anyone else, not so easily. I feel pretty close to you, kid. You're easy to talk to."

The guard opened the door. I stepped out of the cell and he closed the door and locked it. I took a last look at Murray, smiled at him, said something cheerful. Then I walked with the guard along the corridor and down the stairs.

The bastard tipped. Murray tipped, he caught on, he knew. And now, cute as a palmed jack, Murray Roger was playing games of his own.

Well, what else? He had a perfect explanation, a hell of a convincing confession. He was a killer, he couldn't get away with it, he was admitting it and taking the consequences. He had an explanation for everything, even had a way doped out to beat the tax boys and keep them from hanging an evasion rap on him. He told me this, earnest and sincere, and there was only one hang-up.

Because I damn well knew he hadn't killed anybody and he damn well knew it. There were three possibilities—he was crazy, or he was just trying to save his neck. Or finally, he knew. And if that were the case, God alone knew what he was up to. God and Murray Rogers.

I spent the rest of Saturday listening to the radio and dying to tell myself everything was clear and clean and he didn't know a thing. I tried reaching Joyce once. The phone rang and rang and rang and I put the receiver back on the hook and gave up.

My own phone rang that night. It was Barb Lambert. What was I doing? Did I feel like coming over?

I didn't, at first. But there was calmness and softness and warmth in her voice and it reached me. I told her I would pick up a bottle and come over right away. The liquor store around the corner sold me a fifth of Cutty Sark and I drove to Barb's house. We spent the first half hour making a dent in the bottle and becoming comfortable. The comfort didn't last. When I draped an arm over her shoulder I could feel her whole body go slightly tense. I took the arm away and she turned to stare at me.

"Bill—"

"Go on."

"Oh, I don't know," Barb said. "I—what's happening with us, Bill?"

"What do you mean?"

She looked away for a moment or two. Then she said, "You swept me off my feet, you know. I was going along in a quiet little rut and then you came along and changed things. I started caring again. I started to feel alive. I thought you liked me."

"Of course I like you—"

"But things are changing," she said. She was staring at me now, eyes wide, innocent. "You're all wrapped up in something, Bill. You don't really seem to give a damn about me. You slept with me once. Or don't you remember?"

"Barb—"

"But you don't seem to remember. Don't you want to—to sleep with me again? Wasn't I any good?"

I didn't answer her. I stood up, took fresh ice cubes from the silver bucket on the walnut breakfront. I put the ice in our glasses and poured some fresh scotch over the cubes. I set her glass on the coffee table in front of her. She didn't pay any attention to it. I took a long drink and waited.

"I'm shameless," she said. "I like you, Bill."

There were tears welling up in the corners of her eyes but she was determined not to let go of them. She wouldn't cry.

"Bill," she said, "I don't want to be—used. I want to mean something. I want you to like me and to—to love me. I want us to get married, Bill. I'm not in any hurry. But I have to feel that we're moving toward something, not just wandering around in circles. I'm not a kid in college any more. I'm not that young. Do you see?"

"I see."

Her eyes narrowed. "I wish I knew you," she said. "I only wish I knew you. But I don't know you at all."

"Don't be silly."

"Who are you, Bill?"

"You know the answers."

She shook her head very gravely. "No," she said. "No, I don't think so. There's something about you that doesn't make any sense to me. It doesn't fit. I wish I could put my finger on it. You just came to town and slipped into a slot and fitted in perfectly, but there's a part of you that doesn't fit. I—I wish I knew more about you."

"You're making a big thing out of nothing," I said. "I'm just another ordinary Joe, that's all. You can't make me into a romantic figure any more than you can call yourself a call girl. We're ordinary people, Barb."

I tried to kiss her. She pulled away, shaking her head. "Not now," she said.

I finished my drink. She changed the subject, somehow, and we talked for a few moments about trivia. The trivia didn't grasp us all that firmly and the conversation ran out of gas. The silence that followed was uncomfortable, awkward.

Then Barb said, "You can always tell me. Whatever it is, you can tell me, Bill. You know that, don't you?"

"Even if there's nothing to tell?"

Deep eyes cast downward. "There is," she said. "Whatever it is, you can tell me."

14

I spent Sunday night in the little neighborhood tavern where Joyce and I had swigged Black and White and first doped out the way to separate Murray Rogers from his money. I went to the bar sort of by accident. There was dinner in a diner, then aimless driving while the sky went from gray to black in a slow fade. I kept driving, and I worried about Murray and played games guessing how much he knew, and the Ford found that particular bar. There was a handy parking space, I had a thirst. The Ford rolled into the space and I found a stool for myself in the bar.

The same bartender was on duty, the same show on television. I finished one drink and let the bartender pour a new one for me. He took a dollar away and brought back a shiny quarter. I picked it up, held it between the thumb and forefinger of my left hand. I moved my right over it, letting the coin drop into my palm at the last minute. I plucked empty air with my right hand, made a fist.

"Pretty," the bartender said.

I had forgotten he was there. He was looking at my hands with something approaching interest.

"Do it again," he suggested.

"It's nothing."

"Lemme see."

So I did it again.

"Jesus," he said. "Could swear it's there." He tapped my right fist. I opened it, empty, then opened the left one and showed the coin.

"Again," he said. "If I don't see it this time, the house buys a round."

This time I did take the coin in the right hand. He thought he had it cased and tapped the left one. I showed him he was wrong. He clucked admiringly and poured a fresh shot in my glass.

"That's a talent," he said.

"It's nothing."

"It's a real talent," he said. "Try it again for a buck?"

So what the hell. I was quick and smooth this time and when he tapped the left hand I opened it and the right hand at the same time. There was no coin in either hand. He stared at me.

"Try your shirt pocket," I said.

He didn't believe it. But he looked, finally, and there was the quarter, gleaming brightly. It's not a hard move. A little business with the right hand takes his eye out of the picture, and a quick flip from the left hand puts the coin in his pocket. He was leaning forward, so it was easy to drop the coin in without his feeling anything. He shook his head in amazement and gave me a dollar.

"Jesus," he said. "You do this for a living?"

"It's just a hobby."

"You're good at it, though. Real good."

After a while he left me alone. He refocused on the television show and I again lapped at my drink. I sat there and thought about a lot of things. I tried to figure out Murray's angle, and I tried to figure out just how I was going to play things with Barb, and I tried to figure out what the hell I was doing in this town. I didn't come up with any answers. Maybe there weren't any.

On Monday morning Murray Rogers left jail. I was sitting at my desk when the phone rang and Joyce told me he was on his way home. I told her to be careful, she asked of what, and I mumbled something and put the phone down. Be careful of everything, I thought.

I had some calls to make, some people to see. There was a pack of index cards on my desk, all of them typed out neatly and precisely, and there was a long sheet of legal-size yellow paper with a dozen more names and addresses copied down in someone's neat handwriting. I thumbed through the cards and surveyed the yellow sheet of paper and decided I didn't want to call anybody. There were three morning and afternoon appointments listed in my date book. I called two numbers, cancelled out. The third party didn't answer. I shrugged him off and closed my datebook and left the office. I settled behind the wheel and drove about at random. After a while I hit a red light, stopped for it, lit a cigarette with the dashboard lighter.

The job, the life, the world—weren't working. It was a good job, something I could do, something that brought in the money. And it was a good enough life in a good enough world, and for anybody else, maybe, matters would have been fine.

But not for me.

You see, when you're a freelance operator on the periphery of the underworld, you never have to worry about dropping into a bind. You aren't confined, aren't tied down in the least. My business card, if I had one, would go something like this:

WILLIAM MAYNARD
card mechanic and hustler
No Fixed Address

No fixed address. Got a frail hanging on your neck, a broad who won't let you go? Pack your toothbrush, slide into your car, go. Go anywhere because every town has men in it who play cards for money, every town has an angle ready for an angle player. Anybody giving you a hard time? Your room rent overdue? A batch of debts scattered around? Anything like that? Pack the toothbrush, pile in the car, scram.

You start to function in those terms. Even if you're legit—a traveling show biz type, a carnie roustabout, a salesman on the road, an outdoor construction worker—

even then you tend to operate in this manner. You become used to living your life on the move, and when a situation turns sour you run from it and into something better. But if your life runs on illegal tracks to begin with, you find it just that much easier to work this way. Scruples never come along and trip you up. If you're a con man, or a card cheat, or any sort of a thousand hustlers, you're fully accustomed to milking the parks and hunting greener pastures.

Now I was starting to put down roots. A job, sure and steady. A bank account. An apartment with a lease. A circle of friends, most of whom had been born in the area, and who would die there. A girl, a boss, a friend, a friend's wife—

I was in the Ford and the Ford was hurrying along Main Street past Olga Road. A while ago we had crossed Cherry Avenue, the city line around there. If I stayed on Main Street long enough I would wind up in the state capital some three hundred miles away. Or, if I made a right turn in a quarter mile, I could take the big ribbon straight on to New York, a few hundred miles of perfect roadway. I didn't even need my toothbrush. Toothbrushes aren't all that hard to come by, and I had never developed any great sentimental attachment to mine. Just swing the wheel soft right, pick up a ticket at the toll gate—

But I couldn't, and that was the hang-up. Not now, not with Murray's case all up in the air. So far no one had given me much of a second glance. If I skipped town now, someone would start thinking.

I pulled the Ford off the road, lit another cigarette, smoked a little of it. When the traffic thinned out I whipped the Ford around in a U-turn and drove back into town.

I made my apartment in time to answer the phone. I picked it up, said hello, sat down in a chair. It was Murray, and for a second or two the sound of his voice threw me. I'd almost forgotten that he was out of jail now.

"You're a hard man to find," he said. "I tried you at your office. No luck. Been keeping busy?"

"Fairly busy."

"Uh-huh," he said. "Listen, Bill, I'd like to talk to you. Got anything doing right now?"

I didn't, but I had no overwhelming desire to rush over there. "I'll be tied up for an hour or so," I said.

"And after that?"

"I'll be free."

"Good. I'd ask you to come over here, but I'd rather go some place where we can be alone. I'm not under house arrest, you know. I'm just supposed to stay within city limits, something like that. Where can you meet me?"

"Anywhere."

He thought it over for a moment. "There's a little

lunch counter at Washington and Plum," he said. "Sort of a central location, and the coffee's not bad. All right with you?"

"Fine with me."

"About an hour?"

"Right."

"Good," he said. "I'll see you then."

I hung up and found a bottle of Cutty Sark with a little left in it. I poured a small shot and tossed it down. Murray Rogers wanted to see me. I didn't know why.

The hour dawdled along. I smoked a few cigarettes and listened to mood music on the radio. I had another shot of scotch. Then it was time to go. I found Washington and Plum. The lunch counter was diagonally across the street from me on the northwest corner next to a drugstore.

I crossed Washington, waited for a light, crossed Plum. I stepped into the lunch counter and sat down on a plastic-covered stool and leaned on the formica counter. I asked for black coffee and a ham sandwich. The coffee steamed in front of me about the same time Murray appeared.

No jailbird he. He was wearing a suit some expensive tailor had made. There was a fresh white carnation in the buttonhole. His tie had the Countess Mara crest, his shoes had a mirror shine, and the smile on his face would have done justice to an upstate politician. Confident eyes, a firm stride, a quick and strong handshake.

"Sorry I'm late," he said to me. "Just coffee, and black," he told the counterman. He eased himself on to the stool next to me, took a cigar from his jacket pocket, cut the tip, put it in his mouth and lit it. He blew out a cloud of smoke. We both sat there. He watched the smoke and I tried to guess what this was all about.

He said, "Maybe I shouldn't have bothered you, Bill. But I'm worried."

"About what?"

"About Joyce. Have you seen her at all?"

Easy now. "Once or twice, since—"

"Since I was arrested?" I nodded. "Then you probably know what I'm getting at," Murray said. "How did she seem then?"

Anxious to be laid, I thought. And worried that you, Murray, might wiggle off the hook.

"She seemed all right," I said. His eyes were studying my face. "A little—well, worried, of course. But she didn't believe you were guilty and she was sure everything would work itself out."

"Yes," he said. "Yes, of course." He chewed on the cigar, puffed on it, blew out another cloud of smoke. We were riding two levels, I thought suddenly. There was something underneath everything he said, something I could only half hear. "She didn't know I was guilty," he said softly. "That's it right there, in a nutshell. Now she knows."

I didn't have anything to say.

"She's in a bad way, Bill. Maybe she's worrying about what's going to happen to me. Maybe it goes deeper than that. Maybe she can't accept the fact I killed Milani. Whatever it is, it's changed her. And I don't like it."

"How do you mean?"

"She's tense and nervous and depressed. The tension and the nervousness—that's understandable, that's not so dangerous. But the depression bothers me. I'm afraid of it."

"Afraid?"

"Afraid. Afraid she might—might do something rash."

The counterman brought Murray's coffee and my ham sandwich. I took a bite and sipped at my coffee. I put the sandwich down, turned, looked at him.

"I've only been out of jail a few hours," he said. "Maybe things will change. I've tried to perk her up, tried to reassure her that there's nothing to worry about, that Nester figures we have a good chance to get clear on temporary insanity. If she were just worried about me, I could probably talk her out of the mood she's in. But I think there's something else."

"What?"

He took a long sip of coffee. He didn't look at me

when he talked. "Joyce came from a less than ideal background," he said. "I suppose you know that."

"I didn't," I said.

"Well," he said. "At any rate, she's extremely conscious of social position, has been ever since we were married. I'm no psychiatrist, Bill, but I've got enough sense to know she feels insecure in the position she's gained through marriage to me. And now she sees that position as shaky. She thinks we can't hold up our head in this town any longer. She sees her whole world crumbling around her, and the result is a pretty terrifying depression. I'm afraid of it, to tell you the truth. Afraid of what she might do."

I didn't answer him. Everything had a funny ring to it, an odd feeling. I felt as though our roles had been reversed. I was supposed to be the one on the inside while he was swimming in dark waters. But everything was getting scrambled. I had the uncomfortable feeling he knew things I didn't know, and that I was way off in a corner somewhere. Depressed? Anxious about her social position? It didn't sound much like Joyce. Maybe she was putting on an act for his benefit, maybe he just had things ass-backwards. But I couldn't help getting the impression he had somehow taken the ball away from me.

"Bill, I shouldn't have bothered you. I don't know what you can do—"

"That's what I was wondering."

"Unless you could talk to her," he said. "You might have some influence over her."

"Me?"

He nodded. "She seems to think a lot of you. You must have made a good impression on her."

"I hardly know her," I said.

He let that go right on by. "She has a bottle of sleeping pills," he said. "Or had. I—I took them out of the medicine chest, spilled them into the toilet and threw the bottle away. That's how worried I am."

"You don't think—"

"That she'll kill herself? I certainly hope not. But I don't know what to think any more, Bill."

We batted it around for ten or fifteen minutes. The conversation ran out of gas and I made up something about another appointment and having to run. I caught the check, he argued, I paid, he left the tip, we left the restaurant. He crossed to his car and I to mine and that was that. I returned to my office long enough to cancel a couple of appointments and retrieve a few things I wanted from my desk. Perry Carver and I tossed some small talk at each other. Back at my place I broke the seal of a fresh bottle of Cutty Sark. Then I sat in a chair and tried to get some thinking done.

One fact emerged. I was finished with this town and it was finished with me, for all practical purposes. My working for Perry Carver had been a kick at the beginning, more because the job was something new than because of anything else. Now the job wasn't new any more. And jobbing Murray Rogers had been exciting enough in a sort of scummy way, but that too was finished with now. He had been neatly boxed, and whether or not he got off without a jail sentence, Joyce would have what she wanted. She could divorce him with no trouble at all and could pick up a healthy settlement in the process.

And my part of the proceeds? Gone and forgotten, as far as I was concerned. I didn't want Murray's money now and I didn't want Murray's wife. I wanted to do what a grifter does when the setting turns sour. I wanted to take off.

Hell, I could do it. Murray was nailed to his guilty plea, and to Joyce it didn't much matter if I stuck around or not. A day, two days—time to clean out the bank account and pay off the money due on the Ford and straighten myself out with Perry Carver. And then I could leave. No hits, no runs, no errors—well, maybe a few errors, come to think of it. And a great many men left on base.

So I'd drive out Main Street in a day or two, and this time I would take that right turn at the Thruway entrance, and pick up the ticket, and drive the four hundred miles to New York. And after two hours making the rounds of a few right places I would make the proper contacts and work the proper connections and get ready to spend the rest of my life doing what

I was evidently born to do—plucking pigeons and shearing lambs with false shuffles and crimp cuts and hold-outs and second deals.

But there was something I had to take care of first, a bridge that had to be burned correctly. I waited until it was about the right time. Then I picked up the phone and dialed the number.

She answered right away.

"Barbara," I said. "This is Bill."

"Oh," she said.

"Are you busy tonight?"

"No."

"Dinner? I'll pick you up around six?"

"Fine," she said.

I put down the phone and wondered just how I would tell her that she wouldn't be seeing me again.

15

Barbara Lambert was such a very damned fine girl. If she had been aggressive or cheap or mercenary or a nymph or anything like that, then there would have been no need to tell her in the first place and telling her would have constituted no major problem. But she was a very damned fine girl, and I would have no fun telling her we were quits.

I told her at the end of the dinner. We went to the Evergreen and had rare steaks and baked potatoes, and I told her over coffee. I set my cigarette in the enameled ashtray and put my coffee cup in its saucer and spoke her name.

"Go ahead," Barb said.

"Go ahead?"

"Go ahead and tell me," she said.

She was especially attractive that night. The blond hair gleamed, the blue eyes struck sparks, the knit dress was tight around the soft curves of her body. But her lips were set now and her fingers gripped the cigarette she was smoking almost tightly enough to break it in half.

I said, "I'm leaving town in a few days."

"For how long?"

"Permanently."

She didn't say anything. She nodded, digesting the information along with dinner.

"Why, Bill?"

"Reasons."

"Reasons you want to talk about?"

"Well—"

"You don't have to, Bill."

This last said softly, quietly, with the head lowered and the sentence trailing off. "Oh, hell," I said. "It's no great secret. Things aren't working out here, that's all. I'm the old square peg in the round hole, that bit."

"I thought you were doing well."

"In some ways."

She didn't say anything. I waved for the check and put a bill on the table to cover it.

"Come on," I said. "Let's get out of here."

We left the Evergreen. We drove for a couple of blocks without saying anything.

Until I said, "I'm not the guy you think I am, Barb."

"You aren't?"

"No."

"Who are you, then?"

So I shrugged and told her. Not all, of course. Not close to all. But a little, and enough.

"I'm a sort of a criminal," I said. "In a way. A con man, a hustler. I deal in high-priced card games. I'm good with my hands. Sometimes I cheat. Most of the time I cheat."

She didn't say anything. She was staring straight ahead. I offered her a cigarette. She didn't take it.

"I wound up in this town by mistake," I went on. "Things kept falling in my lap."

"Like me?"

"Like you. Like a batch of friendships. Like the job with Black Sand. All of that. I—I hadn't planned on any of that. I was going to stay in this place long enough for Sy to fix my teeth and then I was going to leave. I didn't want to settle down here."

"What changed your mind?"

"I don't know," I said, not entirely dishonestly. "I'm not sure. I guess I thought maybe it could work out, living an honest life, staying in the same place forever."

"But it didn't."

"No," I said. "It didn't."

More silence. I drove on this street and that street and paid very little attention to where I was going. She held out one hand for a cigarette. I gave her one and she lit it herself.

"Where are you going, Bill?"

"I don't know yet."

"Why don't you take me with you?"

"Barb—"

"I'm good company," she said. "I can cook and sew

and say bright things. I'm fun at parties. And I know when to shut up and get out of the way. Most of the time, at least."

I didn't say anything. Barb smoked her cigarette.

She said, "Why not?"

"I can't."

"He travels fastest who travels alone? I won't try to slow you down or cramp your style. I'm not the reformer type. Remember the game we played? I'll be the high-priced call girl type, Bill. I'll live your life." She turned away and I couldn't see her eyes. "I remember playing that game, Bill. Only you weren't playing, and maybe I knew that all along."

"Barb."

She got rid of her cigarette. "No?"

"No."

"You wouldn't even have to marry me or anything. See how shameless I am? You could just take me along. I'll be your private whore, Bill. I'll be William Maynard's private whore. That's quite a little title, isn't it?"

I could see her face again. There were tears in the corners of her eyes. The tears weren't flowing down her cheeks. The tears just stayed there, like pearls, like beads of sweet sweat. She didn't wipe them away. I wanted to stop the car and kiss them away.

"Bill, why won't you take me?"

"Because you don't belong. It's not your life."

"What is?"

"A house. Kids. A good man."

"Aren't you a good man?"

"Not at all."

"Can't I have a bad man?"

"No."

"Why not?"

"Because you wouldn't like it," I said. "Oh, it would be a storybook life for the first little stretch. Then it would turn sour for you. You would get sick of cheap hotel rooms and shabby men and sleeping days and hustling nights. You couldn't take it."

"Because I'm weak?"

"Because you're human. Because you can only function in the gray world when a part of you is missing, Barb. The out-and-out crook is different. He's some kind of a rebel or some kind of a nut or both, and all his lines are clearly drawn. The marginal criminal is in a different boat. He's a human being with a certain part of his humanity surgically removed. He operates differently, functions differently, reacts to different stimuli."

"You talk well for a crook."

"I'm a bright crook. Intelligence doesn't have much to do with it. The smartest man I ever met was a high-rolling crap shooter. He didn't cheat. He knew every percentage on every bet, knew that all almost intuitively. He could beat casinos, and he murdered any money-craps game going. He doubled up and worked tricky combinations and did all this with the speed of an IBM calculator. And the dumbest man I ever met was a pool hustler. He acted better than the Method Kids, but he didn't have a brain in his head. It isn't a matter of brains. It's something deeper, more basic."

"Hearing a different drummer?"

"Something like that."

"And I don't hear that drummer?"

"Be damn glad you don't."

"Why? Because I can live a good clean life?"

"Uh-huh."

"A good clean life," she said. "And when it's all over I'll be just as dead as everyone else."

Two tears spilled over, rolled slowly down either cheek. I moved to wipe them away. She twisted away from me, brushed savagely at the tears with the back of her hand.

"When are you leaving, Bill?"

"A day or two."

"That soon?"

"Just about."

"Oh." She took a breath. "I think you should take me home now, Bill. Please."

I headed the car in that direction. I didn't say anything. Neither did Barb. I did some thinking, and I suppose she did the same, and nothing seemed to add up the way it would have in the movies. In the movies every sucker gets an even break, which is wrong. Runyon had the real story—all of life is six-to-five against.

So I didn't say anything and neither did she. At one point I leaned over and turned on the car radio. Some disc jockey was playing *Two Different Worlds*, proving that there is a God, and that He's equipped with a deadly sense of humor. The record got halfway through the first chorus before Barb reached over to turn it off.

Then we were pulling up in front of her house. She switched off the ignition and pulled up the handbrake. She took the keys out of the ignition and handed them to me.

I looked at her. Calm, now. Cool.

"Come inside with me," she said.

"Barb—"

"Please," she said.

It was soft and warm and wordless. We walked to the door without touching one another. She opened the door with her key. I kept thinking that I shouldn't be here, that I had no right. But she was calling the tune. Inside, she closed the door, and in a moment we were in the bedroom, and she closed that door, too, and turned from me and began taking off all of her clothes.

Nude, she smiled strangely at me. She raised her

hands to her breasts, cupped them, felt of their weight. She let her hands trail lingeringly down the front of her body, touching, displaying. "Look what you're giving up, Bill," she said very softly. "It's not all that bad, is it?"

It wasn't bad at all. I took a step toward her and she choked back a sob and rushed into my arms. I held her and she put her head against any chest and sobbed aloud. I stroked her back and reached down. She pressed herself against me. I reached over and scooped her up and tumbled on the bed with her.

When my hands found her and touched her she was wild. Her feet kicked at the bedclothing and her breasts rose and fell with her furious breathing. I couldn't keep my hands away. I petted her and stroked her until the fire was too much to be borne.

Then we were together.

In bed, she tried to pack a lifetime into a handful of moments. She clutched and held and sought and found. Her mouth was honey-sweet, her breasts cushion-soft, her body a rich vein of warm gold. A lot of sorrow faded and was lost, and a lot of distance melted down and evaporated. There was closeness, and give and take, and something that in a pinch could have passed for love.

Afterward, more silence. She lay motionless on her side with an arm curved under the swell of a breast. Her eyes were closed. She did not move. I bent down and kissed her mouth. I straightened up and tried to think of something to say. Nothing fit. I turned, strode out of the bedroom and out of the house and out of her life.

I drove off with the car radio blaring. I just wanted noise, and static would have served as well as the music. I was tuned to one of those stations that shouts at you. They're supposed to be very big with the teenage set. These stations tell you their call letters every two or three minutes, and they hit you with spot news about pedestrians run down on local streets and kittens rescued from trees and other bits of excitement. I half-listened and half-drove and found a whole load of things I didn't want to think about.

No reason to stay in town. No reason at all. I had found a bad girl, and she had made me do something I shouldn't have done, made me make a big play for the money and the girl—that age-old American dream. I didn't have the money and I didn't have the girl and I didn't even want either of them very much anymore.

And then I'd found another girl, a good girl, and I had to run away and leave her. I didn't want to, but I had to, because that was the only way it would play.

Beautiful.

There was a bottle of Cutty Sark somewhere around the apartment, but I would be alone there, and solitary drinking didn't appeal. I found a bar on Orchard close enough to empty to be reasonably quiet. I sat as far from the jukebox as I could get and I had a couple of drinks. At first I tried to work things out in my mind, but it didn't take me long to see I wasn't going to get anywhere that way. I gave up and let the liquor do the job it was hired for.

A long time ago life had been infinitely simpler. A long time ago, doing magic tricks in third-rate strip joints and fourth-rate hotels with an occasional birthday party or bar mitzvah thrown in. A long time ago, Maynard the Magnificent instead of Wizard the Mechanic. A long time ago.

There was never much in the way of money in those days. There was never the big score, never the feeling of being on the inside of a swinging operation. But it was cleaner then, and fresher, and you never wound up putting yourself in a box. A person can become too hip, too much with it.

The squares have a better time.

Maynard the Old Philosopher. I scooped my change off the bar top and left the tavern. I drove home, parked the car. The drinks had not done their job. I was still sober, and it was a bad time to be sober. I parked the Ford and headed for the apartment.

My key in the lock, turning. And a funny feeling, hard to describe, harder still to explain. A feeling that someone somewhere had taken the play away from me, that I wasn't reading the backs right. Coin your own cliche, brother. An itchy, uncomfortable feeling.

I opened the door.

He was there, in my chair, his hands in his lap and his feet on the floor and his mouth set in a firm thin line. He should have had a gun in his hand, maybe, but he didn't. He just sat there like a boulder and stared at me.

Murray Rogers.

He said, "Close the door."

I didn't move. I read his poker face and I felt the grim hard brittle tension in the air and I stood in place like a statue.

"Close the door," he said. "Come in, close the door, sit down."

I came in, closed the door. I did not sit down.

"Hello," he said. "Hello, you rotten bastard. Hello."

16

I don't remember sitting down. I must have, because I remember being on the couch later on. And listening while Murray Rogers talked.

"You were very damned smooth," he said. "So polished, so clever. And such a thoroughgoing bastard every step of the way. A card cheat. That's a very noble occupation, Maynard."

I didn't say anything. I watched him take a cigar from his breast pocket, trim the end, light the cigar. He shook out the match and dropped it carelessly to the floor. He filled the room with cigar smoke and talked through it.

"You stole money from me with a deck of cards. You cheated me at the poker table and you cheated me at gin rummy. You took my wife to bed. You let me get you a job and introduce you around. And then you framed me for a murder that never happened. You're a very sweet guy, Maynard."

"When did you tip?"

"You mean when did I catch on?"

I nodded.

"You'll have to excuse me, Maynard. I'm not up on

criminal argot. I caught on a few hours before I decided to plead guilty. I knew all about it by the time you visited me in jail. I've known all along." He chewed the cigar. "You seem surprised."

"Why did you plead guilty?"

"Why not?" He shrugged massively. "I hired detectives the day they jailed me. I had one advantage, you know. I knew I was being framed because I knew very well I was innocent. I had the detectives check on Joyce. They turned up something to the effect that she'd been seen with you earlier. I had men run a check on your background, and I had men get a picture of you and show it round to a few people. One of the men they tried it on was the desk clerk at that hotel. He identified you as August Milani, naturally. That made it fairly obvious."

And there, of course, was the whole hang-up in a nutshell, the whole trouble with the frame. We'd built up a house of cards—marked cards, maybe, but just as flimsy. One little push and everything went to hell in a handcar.

"I almost blew up when I found out," he went on. "Viper in my bosom, all of that. The old story of the newfound friend and the younger wife. I could have called the district attorney and tipped him off, and I would have been out of jail in an hour."

"Why didn't you?"

He eyed me carefully. "What would it get me?"

"Freedom."

"Freedom," he echoed. "Yes, I suppose so. And you and Joyce, what would the pair of you have got? A short prison sentence at the most, and even that might have been hard to arrange if you had the foresight to provide yourselves with a top-grade lawyer. I'd have had freedom, Maynard. And no more than that."

He smiled. "Now think that over," he said. "You've played cards with me. I don't play to get even, you know. I play to win."

He stopped talking and the room was still as death. Smoke hovered in the air. I wanted a cigarette but I didn't reach for my pack, as if a false movement might cause him to shoot me. Which was plainly ridiculous—he didn't have a gun. But the atmosphere was like that.

"I play to win," Murray Rogers said again. "Getting out from under a murder rap isn't winning. It's breaking even. Winning is a matter of turning the tables. It wouldn't be enough to see you and Joyce in jail."

I took out a cigarette. I had trouble lighting the match, but I managed it, and I sucked smoke into my lungs and coughed. I blew out the match and flipped it to the floor and took another drag of the cigarette and choked again, coughing spasmodically.

I said, "What do you want, then?"

"I want to see you dead," he said.

*

In Chicago, in the smoky back room where they had caught me dealing seconds, there had been a moment like that one. The moment between accusation and action, between discovery and punishment. A flat, cold, brittle moment, timeless and vacant. And there had been such a moment long ago, ages ago in the second-rate magician days, when a car I was riding in went off the road and rolled twice. That time we had skidded on gravel on the shoulder of the road, and the car had gone into its spin, and I had sat nervelessly and thought I was going to die and wondered how it would feel. That moment ended when we had crashed—I had emerged unscratched, as it had turned out. The moment in Chicago had ended when the hoods had taken away the money and hauled me out into the alley. The moment now, in this town, was like those other two.

"I was going to kill Joyce, too," I heard Murray say. "I had that all set up. Do you remember a conversation we had a little while ago? I told you she was getting despondent, suicidal. Do you remember?"

I remembered.

"That was part of the plan," he said. "I was just planting the idea in a few people's minds. Then it would have been easy enough. All I had to do was tap her over the head with a poker, knock her cold. Then I would pry open her mouth and shovel the Demerol down her throat. It's easy to make an unconscious person swallow something. You flip the pill to the back of the mouth and massage the throat until the person swallows. All I had to do was feed her a bottle of pills and let them carry her off."

"You're not—"

"No."

I closed my eyes and pictured him doing it. Knocking her cold, then popping sleeping pills down her throat. And sitting by her side, waiting with his special kind of patience. Waiting for Joyce to die.

"I decided I wanted her," he said. "I play to win—I keep saying that, but it sums things up. I play to win. I want Joyce." He smiled. "Joyce and I had a long talk tonight," he said. "Joyce will think very carefully before she looks at anyone else. Joyce is going to settle back into the role of loving wife again. She makes a good wife when she puts her mind to it."

He had bought her and paid for her. Now he wanted to go on owning her. I looked at him and my mind searched for an out and I didn't get anywhere. He wasn't even pointing a gun at me. He wasn't even threatening me. He was sitting there, calm and steady, explaining to me just how he had planned to murder his wife and just how he intended to murder me. A big-time tax lawyer, carefully summing up his case for the jury, being quite explicit, filling in all the blanks, dotting the i's and crossing the t's.

"Why tell me this?" I said.

"So you know what's coming. So you can work up a sweat."

"Suppose I go to the police?"

"Go ahead."

At first they would think I was lying. I could prove my story easily enough. And then they would clap me in a cell and leave me there to rot.

"You won't go to the police," he said. "And it wouldn't do you any good if you did. I haven't done anything wrong. I haven't broken a single law. I'll break one when I kill you, but it will be a little late for you to go to the police by then."

"How are you going to kill me from a jail cell?"

He laughed. "I'll never be in jail again. A respectable man who killed a nonentity who was blackmailing him. My plea is temporary insanity. The prosecution has a weak case without a corpse anyway. Don't you think I'll beat the rap?"

He would. Easy.

Silence in a smoky room. I got another cigarette going. My hands were surprisingly steady. I asked him how and when he was going to kill me. Murray smiled. He was enjoying this. It was his show, and he was having fun.

"I haven't decided yet. I'm in no hurry. I've nothing to gain by rushing things. Besides, I want to give you plenty of time to sweat."

"I may be tough to kill."

"I don't think so. You may be tough to find, but I'll manage it. You'll be leaving town, of course. I wonder where you'll run to. Do you remember what Joe Louis used to say? They can run but they can't hide. I'll find you."

"All by yourself?"

"Possibly. I've got all the time in the world. I think I'll give up my law practice, Maynard. The disgrace and all—an understandable move. I don't have to worry about earning a living. And I have a feeling I'll enjoy hunting you down. If the problem becomes too tough I can always hire detectives. Or professional killers. What do you think a couple of pros would charge to murder you, Maynard? Think I could afford it?"

I didn't say anything. He gazed at me, no smile, no frown. Then, slowly, he got to his feet.

"I don't envy you," he said.

I stood up.

"I don't envy you at all. Wherever you go, you'll be waiting for me. Wherever you are, you'll know I'm after you. It will be a temptation for me to prolong it. Except for the fact that I'll never be entirely satisfied until you are dead."

He used that for an exit line. He walked to the door and opened it. I didn't see him out.

I had to wait until morning. Waiting was hell, but there were things that had to be done. I needed money—money from Perry Carver, money from my bank account. I had to give up a few hours for the dough, which didn't mean much in the long run. But it was hell trying to stay in that apartment, trying to sleep, trying to survive until it was time to run.

I had one drink after he left, then left the bottle strictly alone. I packed my suitcases and loaded them into the trunk of the Ford. I took a bath and smoked a lot of cigarettes and tried to sleep and saw right away that it wasn't going to work. I made a cup of coffee, drank it, smoked some more, left the apartment to go to an all-night beanery for a hamburger and more coffee, returned to the apartment and, somehow, God knows how, made it through the night.

Murray was running a bluff, I kept telling myself. He had tipped to everything and wanted me to leave town and work up a sweat. But he wasn't a killer and he wouldn't kill me. It was nothing but a bluff.

Except that I couldn't make myself believe the bluff. I knew the man. I'd spent hours talking with him. I'd played plenty of cards with him. If he were bluffing, I was Marie of Romania.

I appeared at the Black Sand office first thing in the morning. I told Perry as much as I had to tell him. Just that I was leaving town, and leaving right away.

"I just don't get it," Perry Carver said. "If somebody made you a better offer, let me know about it. I'll top it."

"It's not that."

"Then what is it?"

"Wanderlust," I said. "I've got itchy feet, I guess. I've spent my whole life on the move. I thought I could change my style, but it hasn't been working."

"You're making good money," Perry said.

"I know."

"And you'll make better money. Don't you like the city?"

"I like it well enough. I just want to get on the move again."

"Where to?"

"The West Coast," I lied. "San Francisco, probably."

"That's a long way to go for nothing in particular. You've grown close to Murray, haven't you? His troubles on your mind?"

I shrugged.

"Nothing I can do to change your mind, Bill?"

"I'm afraid not," I said.

Perry Carver sighed. My prospect file was on his desk where I had put it. He pulled out a stack of cards and riffled through them unseeingly. For a minute I thought he was going to shuffle them and deal them out. He stuffed them back into the file and regarded me.

"It's the damnedest thing," he said. "You turned out to be the best man to work out in my office in I don't know how long. You've got a real future if you'll stay in one place long enough to become established. Going to stick with the investment business?"

"Probably."

"If you ever want work—"

"Thanks."

Another sigh. "Some day you'll be tired of moving around. Meet the right girl, that sort of thing. It's just a shame it couldn't have happened in this city."

"Yes," I said. "It is."

Afterward, at the bank I sat down with an official and the two of us subtracted my uncashed checks from my bank balance and figured out what I had coming. He asked me if I wanted a cashier's check for the amount, or traveler's checks, or what. I told him cash would do fine. He stared at me as though I were a throwback to pioneer days and told me what teller to see. I saw the teller and took the cash and left. I stopped at the car place and paid the balance due on the Ford.

I headed out Main Street toward the river, picked up the highway, pointed the car eastward and shoved the gas pedal to the floor. I had to force myself not to speed, especially after I reached the Thruway. There you can do five miles an hour over the limit with total impunity, but the red column on the Ford's speedometer kept edging up around seventy-five and I had trouble easing up. I kept telling myself an extra five or ten miles an hour wouldn't do any good. My foot wouldn't listen.

New York would do for a starter, I assured myself. Only for a starter—New York would be the first place Murray Rogers would look and, large as the city is, you can never completely disappear there. But New York was a good place to make a preliminary connection and put some wheels into motion. After that, I could go anywhere.

And Murray could follow me. He had the time and the money and the patience and the incentive. With those four components you can find anyone anywhere. Don't take my word for it. Ask Eichmann.

It had been a pretty little frame while it had lasted. Very neat, very clever. But the frame had been a gamble that had caved in little by little until less than nothing had remained. First the reward had lost its glitter, then the machinery of the frame had lost a few wheels, and finally Murray Rogers had tipped all the way and the whole house of marked cards had fallen in on itself.

Now I was marked for murder.

Somewhere, there was a moral. Not the Golden Rule bit—you can't apply that to life in the shadow world because the Golden Rule cancels out everything.

No, the charm here was a sharper, hipper, dirtier moral.

Like, *Don't gamble.* Stick to your trade—cheat and steal but never take a genuine chance. Don't cheat in a game with professional gamblers—that can result in your teeth being chipped and your thumbs torn out of joint. And don't set a man up for a murder rap. That can kill you.

So I thought about these things for around two hundred miles. At the service area outside of Syracuse I stopped for gas and coffee. I gulped coffee and the Ford gulped Esso and we hit the road again.

It was dark by the time I pulled into New York. I took the Saw Mill exit off the Thruway, picked up the West Side Drive, wound up driving a little too fast through midtown Manhattan. I stuck the Ford into a lot on Ninth Avenue and lugged the bags a block east and two blocks uptown to a third-rate hotel. I signed in as Mr. Floyd Collins of Barnum, Kentucky. I paid cash in advance, undertipped the bellhop, and wound up in a shabby windowless room.

I had bad dreams.

In the morning I washed and shaved and dressed and grabbed breakfast. I made my calls from the restaurant, not through the hotel switchboard. I used up six dimes before I reached the man I wanted. His name was Marty Dreyer.

"This is Maynard," I said.

"Wizard?"

"Right."

"You just hit town? Hey, I heard stories about you, kid. Something about Chicago."

"That was a while ago," I said.

"Uh-huh. What happened?"

"I was stupid," I said.

"That's the damn truth," Marty said. "What I hear, you don't want to go back to Chicago again. Not for awhile, anyway. Maybe never."

"Maybe never. I'm done being stupid, Marty."

"So?"

"I can use some action."

"Yeah?" I waited while he thought it over. "You're damn good," Marty said. "Maybe somebody can use you, Wizard. Meet me at the Senator, Ninety-Sixth and Broadway. The cafeteria. You know the place?"

"I know it."

"Good," Marty said.

17

There was poker, mostly, with a little gin when somebody arranged it. I moved to a different hotel and sold the Ford to a used-car dealer out in Brooklyn. Sometimes, during the tight parts of a game, I forgot all about Murray Rogers. Sometimes. Not often.

Every afternoon at the out-of-town newspaper stand behind the Times Tower I picked up papers. Every afternoon I checked them out. During the third week Murray's case came up for trial. The trial didn't take long, and neither did the jury of his peers. They found him guilty by reason of temporary insanity and let him go. That day there was a picture of him on the back page of the second section, a shot of Murray shaking hands with the foreman of the jury. The tax lawyer also had one arm around an uncertain-looking Joyce. Murray wore a victor's smile. I couldn't help thinking the smile was for me.

Two days later there was mail for me at the hotel desk. I was using the name Robert Lyons, to whom the envelope was addressed. There was the fatal postmark, no return address. I shook all the way upstairs, locked the door and opened the envelope.

Inside, on a piece of plain white paper: "Soon," it said.

Corny as a field in Iowa, melodramatic as *The Perils of Pauline*. I left the room and spent the rest of the day peering over my shoulder to see if anybody were tailing me. I couldn't spot anybody.

That night I took a jet to Cincinnati. I bought my ticket as Howard Foley and registered at a main-stem Cincy hotel as Louis Mapes. Cincy is a quiet town, with all of the action tucked across the river in Newport and Covington. I knew people there. I met one of them and moved into the swing of things.

The hell, Murray had to find me in New York. It was too obvious a place, and I couldn't stay there forever. Newport was safer.

It took Murray ten days. Then another envelope came, addressed to Louis Mapes, postmarked New York. No message. Just a sheet of the same paper, and, folded into it, a small capsule marked Demerol.

I spent close to a month in Seattle. I was a little cuter about it this time. I flew from Cinci to Dallas under one name, caught a jet from Dallas to San Francisco under another, and rode north on a train to Seattle. I didn't even play cards there. I laid low and stayed at the hotel. The money started to thin out, but I figured to stay put long enough for the heat to die down before I tried somewhere else and found a way to make a living.

I started feeling safe again. Murray Rogers was a human being, not a superman. He wasn't even a particularly knowledgeable individual when it came to my side of life. He was a solid citizen, a mark, a square. He had stuck with me neatly, but now I had slipped him and he would stay lost. I was safe.

Until the letter came. More corn—an advertisement for an east coast funeral home enclosed in an envelope postmarked Los Angeles. I threw it away. I sweated. I called the desk and asked them to send up a bottle of Cutty Sark, and I sat on the edge of the bed drinking the scotch. Murray Rogers just didn't give up. He just wouldn't get lost.

So many cities. East, west, north, south—after a while each of the cities is pretty much the same. The weather is different and the names are different and the hotel rooms vary somewhat, but in time these subtle distinctions blur and it's all one town, all one room.

In Kansas City, a truck backfired while I was strolling down the street. I fell to the ground and waited for the second shot. It didn't come, of course. People looked at me as though I were crazy.

Maybe I was.

Running, always running. Running frenetically from a heavyset tax lawyer with nothing in the world but plenty of money and plenty of time, plenty of patience and plenty of drive.

Running.

You run for so long and then the string spins out. The money goes, but the money is only a very small part of the scene. You become tired, so very damned tired, and you run and run and search for a way out, and there isn't one.

I read once about some psychologists who taught rats to solve mazes. Then the psychologists put the rodents in mazes with no exit. The animals scurried around and did their best. Then they sat down and chewed off their own feet.

I can understand why.

In Dayton, I wound up in a five-a-week furnished room on Webster off Payne. I hadn't heard from Murray in a long time, but I knew he was close. I could sense it.

I left the room one day and, when I returned, there were two men waiting, a big one and a small one. I opened the door and saw them and knew what they were there for. I tried to duck out but the big man blocked my path. I struck out ahead and the little one swung a leather-covered sap at my head, and all the lights blacked out.

I came to in a fast-moving car, the little man at the wheel. I hadn't expected to wake up. I started to say something but the big man spoke first. "Somebody wants to see you," he said. "We better keep you nice and quiet in the meantime."

A needle pricked my skin, a shot of something potent. Everything faded to black again and I slept.

It was a long ride. I woke up five or six times, and each time I got another taste of the needle and slept some more. When we reached our destination I was semiconscious. They parked the car and carried me from the car to the house, the big man lifting me effortlessly, like a sack of dirty laundry. I felt like a sack of dirty laundry, as far as that goes. Dirty and damp and a little mildewed around the edges.

I blacked out again. I came to in a chair, an easy chair. I opened my eyes and blinked. I was in the basement of Murray's house. The big man and the small man stood over to one side. Joyce, her eyes terrible, was sitting on a couch along the far wall.

There was a table, two chairs. There was a score pad and a deck of cards and a gun that looked as big as a cannon.

Murray Rogers was sitting in one of those chairs.

"Well," he said. "Hello, Maynard. It's been a long time."

"Go ahead," I said.

Murray's smile grew.

"Go ahead and get it over with," I told him. "You've got a gun this time. Pick it up and shoot me."

"Just like that?"

"You might as well," I said. "I can't run any more.

I couldn't hide well enough. Every damned time I thought I was clear you turned up on my tail again. I've had the course. Get it over with."

The room stayed silent for a long time. I remembered my first visit to that basement game room, that first poker game, that first look at Joyce. It seemed so long ago.

"These past few months have been quite an experience for me," Murray said. For me, too, I thought. "The role of the hunter is an interesting one," he resumed. "It's not without its moments. There's a story called *The Most Dangerous Game*, about a crack hunter who grows bored with the sport and hunts men instead. You probably haven't read it—"

I'd read the story. Just because a man is a crook people tend to assume he's illiterate as well.

"—but I can understand that story now," Murray continued. "You know, at first I planned to chase you and let you run and chase you some more and then kill you."

"And?"

"There's not enough sport there," he said. "I've got a better idea. We played some cards together, Maynard. Gin, poker. You won when you wanted to win. You're quite a good card cheat, aren't you?"

"Good enough."

"Very good indeed. You know, after I found out about you there was one question that kept nagging at me. I suppose it always comes up in connection with a card cheat. I wondered how good a game you might play if you had to play it honest."

I'd wondered the same thing myself, naturally. I'd never been forced to find out. If I were under pressure to win, I cheated. If I were just playing for the hell of it, I could afford to play a sloppy game.

"Get to the point," I said.

"The point ought to be clear enough." He stood up, stepped toward me. "I could have you killed right now. These men—" he indicated the tall one and the short one, my Mutt and Jeff friends "—these men would kill you if I told them to. Kill you quickly and easily and toss you in a lime pit somewhere on the lake shore. All I have to do is give them the word. But I'm offering you a chance. We're going to sit down at that table, you and I. We're going to play gin rummy. We'll play ten sets of Hollywood, the usual rules. And you won't cheat."

"How would you know if I did?"

"I could tell."

"You never knew the difference before."

His eyes flashed—he hated to be a sucker, and I was reaching him. "I never looked for it before," he said. "I trusted you, you bastard. This time I'll be looking. So will the boys. If you cheat, you die on the spot. And badly."

"Go on."

"If you win, if you beat me fair and square, you pick up all of the marbles, Maynard. All of them."

"What does that mean?"

"It means fifty thousand dollars in cash. It means Joyce. She can go with you, if you want her. I won't be in your way."

I glanced at Joyce. She was more beautiful than ever, but there was something wrong with her, something in her eyes. Before she had been vital and alive. Now, somewhere in the course of things, Murray had taken the spirit out of her. It showed.

I said, "And if I lose?"

"Then you die."

I nodded slowly. It was as corny as some of his other slants, as corny as sending me funeral home advertisements through the mail. He had a real feeling for melodrama. But there was plenty underneath that layer of corn.

He couldn't stand being a loser. And he couldn't stand the idea I might be able to beat him in a straight game just as I'd beaten him cheating. Gin was his game. He was good at it, just as he was good at so many other things, and he was sure he could take me. When he did, it would cost me my life.

I've never been much of a gambler on the square. Cheating isn't gambling. It's a sure thing. I never liked to bet big money on horses or dice. And I never thought I'd wind up betting my life on a gin game.

"Well? Is it a deal?" he said.

A hell of a deal, I thought. What happened if I said no? Then I just died anyway.

"The way things sit," I said, "you've got the cards stacked in your favor."

"How?"

"I'm half-dead and half-drugged," I said. "My mind's not working straight and my body's crapping out on me. I'll play your game, but I've got to be in shape for it."

That made sense to him. If I weren't at the top of my form, it therefore would be no victory for him. He asked me what I wanted.

"First a shower," I said. "Then about four hours in the sack. Then a lot of scrambled eggs and a pot of black coffee, and a thermos of coffee on the table throughout the game. And a few packs of my brand of cigarettes."

"Is that all?"

"That's all."

"Good enough," he said.

I took the shower and hit the sack. I woke up by myself about fifteen minutes before my four hours were up. There was a change of clothing laid out for me. My size. I dressed, ate half a dozen eggs with bacon and drank four cups of inky black coffee.

I went downstairs, and Murray was at the table waiting for me. The gold-dust twins were down there, too. They were going to help watch me to make sure I didn't cheat. Between them, they had maybe three fifths of a brain.

"Our regular rules," Murray said. "Hollywood, spades doubled, ten for underknock, twenty for gin, thirty for gin-off. We'll play ten sets with no break until we're finished."

"Fine."

He broke open a deck of cards, passed them to me. I flipped through them to see if they were readers. They weren't.

"Cut," he said.

I cut a seven, he cut a jack. He dealt.

Murray Rogers took the first set clear, with a blitz in the third game. I couldn't keep my mind on the cards the way you have to. My head wasn't working right. I drank coffee until my teeth were floating, and I buckled down and riveted my mind to the game. I forgot the money I'd have if I won and I forgot the bullet I'd win if I lost. I concentrated on the cards.

And I played him, too. You can get hurt in gin if you just play the cards on the table. You have to play the person as well. You have to tip your opponent off balance, to smart under his skin so that he begins to make mistakes. It's a war of attrition and nerves, and you have to handle yourself just right.

On the second set, I softened Murray up with a

series of fast knocks. The brand of gin we were playing was stacked against the quick knock. All the bonus boxes came for going gin, and a knocker was going to a lot of trouble to make a damned few points.

But I was softening him up. I went down quick five hands in a row and I was setting up a pattern. The sixth hand, I drew very good cards right from the gun. It was a spade hand, too. I sat there like a stone, and Murray made his bid for the only good defense against a fast knock. He got down fast himself, and he knocked before I did, with eight points in his hand.

I was sitting with one loose card, a six of hearts that played off against a run of his. That made it a gin-off, good for six boxes and sixty points. It put me out in two games and close to out in the third.

We continued that way. He was better at playing gin rummy, but I was damned good at playing Murray Rogers, playing him like a fish on a line. He became lucky and took the third set, and I came back in the fourth and very strong in the fifth. He blitzed me two games out of three in the sixth set. When we finished it I asked for a summary of the score. He tore off a clean score sheet and added up all the figures. With six of ten sets completed, we stood fairly close.

But he was a few hundred points to the good.

I gulped more coffee. We were even enough, I thought. Even on the score and even as far as ability was concerned. Over the long haul, I figured I could probably beat him. If we played gin every day for a year I would win more than I lost.

Fine.

But we had only four more sets to go, and we were evenly matched enough so that anything could happen in four short sets. It could be a simple matter of him winning the spade hands and me winning the regular ones. If he had a little break in the luck department, he would come out on top. And I would wind up in that lime pit on the lake shore.

I was gambling for my life.

And I remembered that moral that had occurred to me on my way to New York. *Don't gamble. Stick to your trade and don't take chances.* My trade was the card mechanic's trade, and here I was staking my life in a straight card game.

It was purely crazy.

There was no question of honor involved, not as far as I could see. He had brought me here by force and he had arranged the game on threat of death. The game was being played on his terms, not mine. And honor had never been my long suit to begin with. I was playing to stay alive, and he was playing to see me dead.

So I started doing what I had always done well.

Gin is a beautiful game for a good mechanic. If you know what you're doing you can cheat on center-stage with every eye on you and still get away with it.

Knowing the position of one card in the deck can make the difference on a hand. Setting up just one or two things can make you a winner every time out.

It was nerve-wracking. The Mutt and Jeff team was sitting in close, never taking their eyes from my hands. But we had been playing for a long time and the boys had watched for a long time without seeing anything remarkable. They were tired, and they weren't as sharp as they might have been. And Murray was under enough pressure so that he couldn't watch me all that close and still pay full attention to his cards. He had to study the cards to beat me, and that gave me just enough room to swing.

I won the seventh set big. I knew the bottom three cards in the deck every time I dealt, and that's a big edge—when you know what you don't have to look for, when you know what cards are out of the hand, you've got a healthy advantage. And this was a kind of cheating no one could pin down. All I did was manage to see those bottom cards in the course of the deal. I didn't move anything or stack anything, just managed a peek.

There were other tricks. On one hand, I went for an early knock. I had a lay of four kings in my hand. When I scooped up the cards for the deal, I made sure those four cowboys wound up all together on the bottom of the deck. They stayed there during the shuffles, until the last shuffle when they wound up all in a row about a third of the way up from the bottom. When Murray cut, the kings were grouped among the first twenty cards.

He got a pair and I got a pair. Fair enough. Only I knew what Murray was holding and he didn't know what I held. All I had to do was wait. He couldn't do anything as long as he held on to the kings because I wasn't about to break up mine. And when he did break his, finally, I picked up his discard and ginned with it. That happened to come on a spade hand, too, and it put me out in two games.

I won two games of the eighth set and he came back and won the other. With two sets to go, the tables had turned a little. I was three hundred points out in front.

"You're luck's getting better," Murray said.

"It's not luck. I'm outplaying you."

"You bastard," he said.

I kept the needle in. "You don't play a bad game," I said, "but you're not flexible enough."

"Shut up and deal."

"I want more coffee."

One of the heavies ambled for coffee. I shuffled the cards and kept up a running stream of chatter until I had a cup of mud at my elbow. I drank it down and dealt out the hands. By this time he was so tensed up that I beat hell out of him without cheating at all.

Then, toward the end of the ninth set, he hit a streak of pretty luck. He was doing everything right and I couldn't get to him. We had just broken open the eighth new deck of cards, and he couldn't seem to lose with them.

I won a hand, finally. And I shuffled the cards and stopped suddenly and boxed them and looked through them.

He had brought in a deck of readers.

I glanced up at him. He had a sick look on his face. I called the cards off one at a time, then turned them face up. I called ten cards right in a row. They were Bee brand, the diamond back design, and the markings were in the little diamonds near the corners.

Marked cards are strictly for amateurs. A pro never uses anything phony—he gets by on his own abilities at sleight-of-hand and misdirection. Whenever you see daub or marked cards or luminous readers or hold-out machines, you know you are dealing with a wiseass amateur looking for the best of it.

"These are your cards," I said.

"I—"

"They came in at the beginning of this set," I said. "I think we ought to forget this set and go back to the end of the eighth. I think we ought to play two more sets with straight cards."

He just nodded.

From there on in I didn't have to cheat. He was beaten all the way. Even when the cards ran his way he couldn't do things right. He had tried to do some cheating on his own hook, and he had been caught at it, and he was through. On the tenth and final set I blitzed him three games straight. The bastard never won a hand.

Murray sent the boys away. He gazed at me and his shoulders sagged. "You win," he said. "It's all yours. Fifty thousand dollars. And Joyce, if you want her."

I turned to her. As desirable as ever, unless you saw the death in her eyes.

"I don't want her," I said.

Murray was tremendously relieved. Then he said. "The money—"

"I don't want the money, either," I said. I pushed back my chair and turned away from him. I didn't want to look at either Murray Rogers or Joyce now.

I got out of there and closed the door.

I traveled as far as a drug store and called a cab from there. He travels fastest who travels alone, I thought. But I wasn't in such a hurry now. There were more important things than traveling fast.

The cabby found the high school and let me off in front of it. In the lobby a girl with straight hair and braces on her teeth told me how to find Mrs. Lambert's classroom.

Barb was standing at the blackboard with a piece of chalk in her hand. She looked as fresh and sweet as a mouthwash ad. I stood in the doorway for a few seconds and gazed at her. She didn't see me.

I thought, Jesus, go away, leave her alone.

But I stepped into the room and she turned and stared.

And I said, "Did you mean it? The whole whither-thou-goest routine?"

"I meant it."

"All the way?"

"All the way. Bill, I—"

"Have you a car outside?"

"Yes," Barb said.

"Are you ready to go?"

"I'll have to pack. I—"

"No time. You can buy things."

The kids in that class could never have understood. They sat there with their eyes bulging out of their heads while I took her by the elbow and steered her out of the room. We rushed past everybody and into her car and got going. We were on the road.

"This is crazy," Barb said.

"I know."

"All my clothes and everything. And just rushing away like this. Maybe we ought to stop."

"We'll stop."

"We will?"

"Sure," I said. "As soon as I find a motel."

So here we are. The town is Phoenix, although we're never in one town long enough for it to matter too very much where we are. And Barb's last name is Maynard, thanks to a Baptist Minister in Orchard Falls. But she uses her maiden name in the act.

The act is nothing too very special. We're playing a small club called the Desert Points now. I'm Maynard the Magnificent, deft and agile as always, and Barb is my assistant, the girl I saw in half, the girl who drags out the prop wagon and enchants the customers with her mammary development. We go on before the stripper and after the female impersonator. We're not exactly the World's Fair, but we like it.

Sometimes I meet someone who knows me as Wizard. Once in a while somebody from the bad old days wants to know if I still like to take a crooked hand in a crooked game. I don't. Some of them discourage easy and some of them try to push, but they all give up sooner or later.

The money is nothing exciting and the life itself is chaotic and uncertain. But we like it. Barb doesn't seem to care about heavy furniture or charge accounts. There will be a kid or two some day, but we figure they can get used to the life. They may miss out on some schooling, but they'll learn their geography first-hand. And they'll be pulling rabbits out of hats before they're toilet-trained.

It could be worse. Hell, it has been worse.

It's never been better.

THE
END